Bir

Wilderness

Also by Kate Elizabeth Ernest

Hope Leaves Jamaica

Festus and Felix

for younger readers

Tricky Tricky Twins

Kate Elizabeth Ernest

Birds in the Wilderness

mammoth

For my dear grandmother Carmel
and for my father

First published in Great Britain 1995
by Methuen Children's Books Ltd
Published 1997 by Mammoth
an imprint of Reed International Books Ltd
Michelin House, 81 Fulham Road, London SW3 6RB
and Auckland and Melbourne

ISBN 0 7497 2779 9

10 9 8 7 6 5 4 3 2 1

A CIP catalogue record for this title
is available from the British Library

Printed and bound in Great Britain
by Cox & Wyman Ltd, Reading, Berkshire

Contents

Foreword

In the 1950s and 1960s many West Indians journeyed to Britain seeking 'a better break'. After they had settled, found jobs and homes, they sent for their children who'd been left in the loving care of grandparents and other relatives. The transition from a West Indian childhood to life in a different environment was a culture shock. *Birds in the Wilderness* continues the story of *Hope Leaves Jamaica* and begins in the autumn of 1968.

Welcome to the Country

We children had thought aeroplanes were big silver birds which flew in the sky. Now we knew better. We had arrived in England by plane on a foggy autumn morning. The fog was so thick we couldn't see the vehicles ahead of us, only the headlights of oncoming traffic, as we travelled along the motorway in a Vauxhall Victor, Father's car.

We knew not what to make of Father. He was a tall man in a big overcoat and trilby. He looked so different from the image I had carried of him: I had expected to see a tall, smiling, wide-shouldered man but now I saw his shoulders were hunched up under the weight of I knew not what. He kept looking over his shoulder at us, taking his eyes off the road. We stared ahead into the vast sea of headlights. The car windows steamed up with our breath. The fog dragged our spirits down.

'Welcome to the country, children,' Father said for the umpteenth time. 'Though I must say this fog is not exactly welcoming.'

'The English weather is unpredictable.' Mother took the chamois leather from the dashboard and wiped the windscreen. She wore a hairy-looking coat, reminding me of a she-goat. She turned and smiled at us. 'I wanted you children to get a glimpse of London, but this fog means business.'

I was tired and all I wanted was a familiar environment. I wanted to go home to Grandma and Grandpa. There was a deep ache in my stomach and each time I thought of them my heart leapt, trying to jump out of my mouth. Meantime, Ruth and Joshua huddled together, drawing warmth and comfort from each other. It was a bleak day.

'Together at last,' Father said.

We remained silent. What were we supposed to say? Father stared ahead.

'Tell me something, children; have you forgotten your mother and me? You haven't said a word since the stewardess handed you over to us at Heathrow. Did you have a good flight?'

We nodded, heads bobbing like puppets. It seemed we children had slept for most of the flight, crying ourselves to sleep. The yellow-haired stewardess had wrapped blankets around us during the night. When the plane landed, she took us to the arrivals area where we stared in amazement at the multitude of white faces; we'd never seen so many white faces before. Our cardboard suitcases looked shabby compared with the beautiful cases being wheeled on trolleys.

The car park at Heathrow was frightening. There was a build-up of traffic leaving the airport, caused by the fog. Drivers were impatient: they honked their horns and revved the engines; the noise irritated our sensitive ears. We crossed the car park nervously; we were convinced we were about to lose our lives.

'Together at last,' Father repeated.

We nodded again.

Mother gave a big sigh. 'Jet lag, I suppose. They've had a long, tiring flight. They'll be more talkative once they've rested and had a good meal.'

'Mm.' Father adjusted the driving mirror. I could see him looking at us. He sighed. 'Autumn is not a good time to arrive in England: the leaves are brown, the birds fly away, the grass is brown; everything is damp and dreary, and to top it all we've got this awful fog.'

'Lord, I miss the sun.' Mother shivered.

I had seen fog before, but nothing prepared me for the blanket shrouding London. The air was heavy with danger and disappointment. Father drove at a snail's pace and the windscreen wipers moved slowly, sending us off to sleep. We dreamed of another place, where thick fog and motor vehicles with blaring headlights were unknown.

'Home at last.' Father turned into a narrow street. We opened our eyes, yawned, reluctantly left the safety of the car and stood on the pavement. The fog was fast disappearing, rising over chimney tops. Net curtains parted and we saw white faces peering at us.

'It's spitting.' Mother stretched out a hand.

We didn't understand.

'Rain.' Father looked up. 'It's drizzling.'

'There's no gold.' Joshua looked down, side-stepped dog's do-do. 'I thought the streets of London were paved with gold.'

'And where's the river?' Ruth interrupted. 'I thought our house was built on the River Thames!'

'Now you know how Dick Whittington felt,' Father said.

9

Rows of houses stood on either side of the street. Smoke curled upwards, rising from the chimneys. We'd seen chimneys in books, we recognised them. Numerous cars were parked outside the houses. We'd never seen so many cars before. I thought of the village square, saw the horses, mules, donkeys.

A man rode past on a horse-drawn cart, ringing a bell. He sang gaily: 'Any old iron, any old iron . . .' He reined in the horses, jumped down, walked over to the kerb and picked up an old cooker. He placed it on the cart, which was loaded with junk. Then he came towards us, smiling. 'Don't suppose you want to get rid of those old cardboard suitcases, mister?'

'No!' Father held our grips tightly.

'Just come off the boat, 'ave they?' he asked.

'No, they flew over: BOAC,' Father said.

'Fancy leaving the sun for this cold climate.'

We just stood there staring at the old man: he looked as if he needed a good shave, a haircut and a bath. We couldn't believe our eyes; we thought everyone in England was rich, clean and tidy.

'Beats me why you coloured people keep coming.' He gave a throaty cough and spat. Then he moved off.

'He spat on the ground,' Ruth said. 'I don't believe it!'

Father slammed the car door. 'Some people have no home-training, no manners whatsoever.'

'Come along, children,' Mother said. 'Take no notice.'

'Er, mister!' A thin voice came from across the road. 'I've got an old fridge for you.' We turned to see a skinny white woman standing on the pavement. Big sponge rollers were stuck into her hair. She wore a floral, orange-coloured apron; there was a cigarette in the corner of her mouth. 'Those yer kids?' she nodded to Mother.

'Yes.' Mother gave a wide smile. It was a matter of her cheeks moving upwards, her mouth opening mechanically, showing her teeth. It died down as quickly as it flared up. She fiddled in her handbag. 'Where are my keys? Let's go inside, children, before Mrs Nosey Parker comes out again.'

The door slammed behind us and we were plunged into darkness. Then Father flicked a switch and the hallway was flooded with light. We children squinted, looking at the electric light bulb in awe; instant light took some getting used to, as did the patterned carpet and floral wallpaper.

Father showed us into the sitting-room and we silently took in our surroundings: we were in a large room where the floral wallpaper and patterned carpet still dazzled our eyes. The room contained an old-fashioned radiogram, a television, black leather-look sofa and a wooden coffee table in the centre. There was a vase of artificial flowers on the table. I sniffed, imagining the scent of fresh flowers. All I could detect was stale cooking and detergent.

'You children must be starving,' Mother said. 'We'll be having fish 'n' chips for lunch, quick and easy. I made it this morning.'

'Fish 'n' chips?' Joshua repeated. 'I don't like fish.'

Ruth touched the stiff-looking flowers on the

11

coffee table. 'Plastic flowers! We have real flowers back home.'

For some reason we children were behaving badly. We should have been happy to see our parents, happy to be in our new home, eager to settle down, but we couldn't help ourselves: we wanted our grandparents and the safety of our cosy cottage back home. We felt miserable, we were bad-tempered.

Father smiled patiently. 'Real flowers are expensive.'

'Look at my baby.' Mother hugged Joshua. 'My little baby . . .' She almost smothered Joshua. He stood as stiff as a board, wearing a miserable face.

Ruth stared at the floral carpet. 'You've covered up the floor. I like polished floor, like Grandma's floor.'

'My, my, you're critical,' Father said. 'Whatever happened to the lovely little girl who used to pleat my handkerchiefs and put them in my pockets?'

'You remembered!' Ruth wore a broad smile. 'I thought you'd forgotten. Fancy that.'

'No way, Princess.' Father lifted Ruth off her feet. He tickled her underarm. 'How could I forget . . .'

'Daddy, Daddy, you're making me laugh,' Ruth screamed with delight. 'Oh, Daddy.'

'My princess.' Father hugged her.

There I stood, completely out of the picture: I felt like the excess baggage at the airport. Mother sat Joshua on her knee, stroking his cropped hair, saying, 'My baby has grown so much. Why, the last time I saw you, you were knee-high.'

I could have cried out in frustration, 'What about

me?' I thought to myself: I don't belong here. I'm too old to sit on Mother's knee, too tall to be lifted and tickled by Father.

'Hope, Hope . . .' Father settled Ruth on her feet. 'How's my little Hope. You look so . . .' He looked me up and down. 'Our little Hope has grown up, Bea.'

Mother put Joshua down, stood with open arms. 'My children have grown. I hardly recognise them.' She sniffed. 'I shouldn't have left them, Jasper. I've missed out on so much. My children don't even know their real mother . . .'

'Hush, hush,' Father said. 'There are many parents in our shoes. We're not alone.'

We children felt guilty. We had made our mother cry. We hung our heads in shame.

'How are the folks back home?' Mother asked. 'Did they send any rum for your father?'

'Yes,' Father said. 'How are they keeping?'

'They are very well, mam, sir,' I said. 'And they said to say "howdy-do". They've sent serosee bush, afo yams, sweet potatoes, ginger, bissy and white rum for you and Mother, sir.'

'Sir, mam!' Father repeated. 'Come, come, Hope. You can do better than that; call us Mum and Dad.'

'Sorry, sir; Dad,' I said.

'My goodness,' Father said. 'I'm a stranger to my own children. We should never have left them for so long, Bea.'

Now it was Mother's turn to console Father. She said, 'Never mind, Jasper. The children are suffering from jet lag. Once they've rested they'll be all right.'

'My children,' Father said sadly. 'What happened

13

to the children I used to know? I'm a stranger to them now.'

I couldn't bury my face in Father's overcoat and tell him how much I'd missed him. I couldn't embrace Mother either. There were no familiar smells, no familiar habits, nothing to bind me to them. I had thought the moment I set eyes on my parents I would fling myself onto them, hugging them and crying at the same time. But the ties that bind parents and children were broken long ago. There was a sense of being in the wrong place with the wrong parents. All the love I bore was left in our cottage back home with my grandparents.

Father had dark watery eyes. He bore his disappointment hard. There was a chill in the room. The happy-go-lucky man, who used to sit me on the bonnet of his Chevrolet on Sundays in Kingston when I was small, was gone for ever.

'Light the gas fire, Bea,' Father said. 'Cold in here.'

Instant heat was a miracle. Joshua knelt by the fire, warming his hands. Ruth sat in front of the fire, shoes and socks off, wriggling her toes.

'You'll get chilblains,' Mother said.

'What are they?' Ruth asked.

'I can see you children have a lot to learn,' Father said.

'Time for lunch,' Mother said. 'Then I'll go and fetch Naomi. Our neighbour, Mrs Parsons, is baby-sitting her.'

'I can't wait to see her,' Ruth said. 'A baby sister . . .'

'That's the spirit,' Father said with relief.

The room was stuffy. The family occupied space as if each had been assigned a place. I sniffed, said the wrong thing. 'I could do with some fresh air, like back home.'

'Back home!' Father repeated. 'Can't you children think of anything else to say?'

There was an awkward silence. Mother sighed. 'Who's for lunch?' She gave Father a stern 'be patient' look.

'Where's the toilet?' Joshua asked. 'I want to wee-wee.'

Lunch forgotten. The house came alive with laughter. Our parents laughed at the repetition 'wee-wee'. We walked up a flight of stairs, saying: 'An upstairs, downstairs house.'

Ruth and Joshua insisted on sliding down the banister, giggling. Afterwards they kept pulling the chain in the loo, laughing each time the water came gushing down. I watched the water swirling round and round in the bowl with fascination.

'Come, come, children,' Father said. 'Don't waste water. Think of the people back home who have to carry water from the public tank or the spring.'

'You just said "back home", Daddy,' Ruth said.

'Yes,' Father said. 'It's a phrase you can't get rid of.'

'Come and wash your hands in the bathroom, children,' Mother said. 'Wait till you see the bath, hot water on tap.'

'Real running water!' Joshua exclaimed.

'No more bath-pan and washstand,' Ruth said. 'A real bath and hot water!'

'Can we see the garden now?' Joshua asked.

15

'Have you got starapple trees, mango trees?' Ruth asked.

Father developed frown lines. 'Let's leave the garden till the fog has cleared properly.' He turned to Mother. 'Why don't you pop next door and collect Naomi?'

'Better still, I'll call Bunty from the garden wall and tell her to bring Naomi over,' Mother said. 'I'm sure the children are longing to meet their baby sister.'

Who's Bunty? I thought, as we went from room to room, exploring the house with wide amazed eyes: electricity and running water under the same roof. We went around switching the lights on and off, running the taps in the bathroom and kitchen, laughing at the tops of our voices. We forgot the bleakness outside. But I sensed the real problem lay ahead of us; I shut it out.

2

Twinkle, Twinkle, Little Star

Click, click . . . Mother's stiletto heels echoed on
the polished floor as we crossed the assembly hall.
We were being escorted by a Sergeant-Major-type
nun in flat, brown, lace-up shoes. Her face was
framed by a black veil. Her name was Sister
Martha. She took long strides and we had trouble
keeping up with her. There was the sound of
giggling in the hall. It was PE time. There were
twenty-odd girls present. They climbed ropes,
jumped over a wooden horse or bent to touch their
toes.

'Girls, girls.' A tall nun wearing a bottle-green
tracksuit and a black veil clapped. 'Pay attention!'

They were looking at us. I was afraid I would
trip up.

'We like our girls to be fit in body, mind and
spirit,' Sister Martha said.

I was still conscious of Mother's heels clicking on
the wooden floor. Mercifully we entered a corridor
which led to a small office. There were posters
of religious people on the wall, including one by
Murillo: The Virgin and Child. Who was Murillo?
There was a wooden crucifix, too. There were
shelves stacked with books. There was an ancient
wooden desk, neatly arranged with papers, an ink-
well and a string of rosary beads.

'Our visitors are here, Sister Bernadette.' Sister Martha bowed and left the room.

'Welcome, welcome . . .' Sister Bernadette had been looking out of the window. 'Now and again the pigeons that live under the railway bridge visit me. They like to sit on the window-sill cooing,' the tall pale-skinned nun said. 'Do sit down.'

'Good morning, Sister,' Mother and I chorused.

'Good morning,' Sister Bernadette said. 'Well, Hope, I expect you're a wee bit homesick.'

I sat with my hands folded in my lap. 'Yes, Sister Bernadette,' I said. 'I miss my grandparents.'

Mother sat stiffly.

'It's to be expected, my child,' Sister Bernadette said. 'Believe me, I know how you feel. When I came over from Ireland as a novice I felt terribly homesick, missed my family and friends; I kept wondering about my vocation . . . Yes, well . . .' She stiffened as though the memory was too painful. 'Time is a great healer.' She became serious. 'Our mission here at St William's is to spread the Catholic Gospel . . .'

'Don't worry, Sister Bernadette,' Mother said. 'Hope is a good girl. She will make a good Catholic.'

I wrestled within. I didn't want to be 'a good Catholic'. Nobody had asked my opinion. Father insisted we children converted to Catholicism. He frowned on the local comprehensives: they were overcrowded with girls who smoked, swore in public, behaved like rowdies on the buses. They had no respect for their elders, let alone their school badges.

'One more thing.' Sister Bernadette reached for her rosary beads. 'Our girls are regular churchgoers. They go to confession on Saturdays, (the younger ones go to catechism on Saturdays), communion on Sundays. I take assembly every Monday morning. I get to know who's skipped communion. I expect them to own up in assembly!'

'No problem, Sister Bernadette,' Mother said. 'Hope will go to church every Sunday. Father Joseph came round to see us last week. He's arranged for Hope and the other children go to catechism on Saturday mornings, followed by confession . . .'

'Good, good.' Sister Bernadette fingered her beads. 'Any questions, Mrs Byfield?'

Mother stuttered, 'I – I think you've said it all, Sister.'

Mother was somewhat intimidated by Sister Bernadette. She had never addressed a Mother Superior figure until then. The air of authority unsettled her. 'No questions, Sister!'

'Very well.' Sister Bernadette looked at her watch. The door knocked. 'Ah, Sister Martha, could you please show Hope and Mrs Byfield around.' She added, 'I look forward to seeing you in assembly on Monday, Hope.'

'Thank you, Sister Bernadette,' I said.

Sister Martha showed us around: there was a needlework room in a kind of attic. Girls sat with heads bent over the electric sewing machines. In the cookery room the girls baked fairy cakes. Some of the girls had red cheeks, partly caused by the heat and partly by our presence. In the art room children sketched with charcoal, some experimented with paintbrushes. As we toured the building I noticed that there were very few black children in the school. I was anxious to leave, especially since Sister Martha kept introducing me as 'the new girl from Jamaica'. My face burned with embarrassment as if it had been set ablaze.

That night I tossed and turned in bed. I didn't want to go to school. I didn't want to convert to Catholicism. I dreamed of Great-Aunt Minnie. I was standing in Uncle Isaiah's sitting-room where Great-Aunt Minnie sat in her high-backed chair. I had flown back to Jamaica. I had no money and I couldn't find my grandparents. I held a faded photograph of Grandma and the ladies in the church choir. Something was wrong. Great-Aunt Minnie was young and bright-eyed. She could see me perfectly well.

'Hope,' she said, 'you can't keep coming home, child. If you are to settle in foreign, you must cast the past aside and embrace the future. Go forward. Shine like a star.'

'Shine like a star . . .' I repeated.

'Ah, child,' she said. 'Leave the past alone and go forward. Shine like a star.'

'I don't understand,' I said.

'One day you will,' she said. 'Now pass me that lamp.' Her fingers were long and smooth. Her teeth were white.

There was an oil-lamp on the table. I fetched it. 'Here you are, Aunt Minnie.'

She handed it back to me. 'This little light of

mine will light the way for you. You've got a long way to go before you get to where you're going.'

There was a long-drawn-out noise, rather like a baby crying. Great-Aunt Minnie said, 'I've got to go now. It's a hard road to travel and a mighty long way to go . . .'

I cried out, 'Please don't go!'

She was gone. I bolted upright in bed and opened my eyes, heart thumping. Ruth slept soundly by my side. The noise continued. The cats in the neighbourhood were calling out.

Ruth rolled onto her side, groaning. 'Those cats again.'

I patted her shoulder. 'Go to sleep.' She was snoring before I could say another word. I envied Ruth. She never ever lost sleep. She could will herself to sleep just like that. On the other hand, I tossed and turned most nights, clinging to the past, crying for my grandparents.

'Hope, Hope.' The floor-boards creaked. 'Are you awake?'

It was Joshua. He slept badly. He had a tiny room next to ours. The walls closed in on him. He'd been having nightmares since we arrived in England a week ago.

'I dreamed there was a toilet in the middle of my bed,' he said. 'I wish people didn't have to dream.' He shivered. 'I've wet my bed, Hope. Please don't tell on me.'

'Of course not. You can change into one of my pyjamas.'

'What about my pyjamas and sheets?' he whispered. 'Mother is bound to find out.

21

Remember how cross she was yesterday. She said bed-wetting was "for babies and there's only one baby in this house: Naomi." I can't stand Naomi. I wish she'd keep out of my way. She's always getting tangled up round my feet. Mother and Father adore her. I can't stand her.'

'Keep your voice down.' I crossed the room, tip-toeing over to the dressing-table, opening the drawers. 'They do love us, but they have a special love for Naomi. She's grown up with them; we haven't. We've got to get to know them all over again.' I handed him a towel. 'You must promise to stop wetting your bed, Josh.' I helped him out of his pyjamas.

There was a sad-faced boy looking at me, shivering. He dried himself off and put on my pyjamas, saying: 'Honestly, Hope, I do want to stop wetting my bed, but I can't help it. I keep having nightmares and dreaming about back home.'

'You'd better stop dreaming,' I said. 'Mother says she doesn't want you ruining her expensive mattress.'

'Money, money . . .' he snapped. 'That's all I ever hear. Grandma and Grandpa never bothered about money. I wish I was back home with them. I never used to wet my bed.'

Ruth rolled over, mumbling, 'What's the matter, Hope?' She opened her eyes. When she saw Joshua she sat up. 'Another nightmare? What's the matter with you and Hope? You two can't seem to settle down at night.'

'Go to sleep, Joshua.' I said. 'I'll put your

22

bedclothes and pyjamas in the laundry bag as soon as we wake up.'

'Thanks.' He climbed into bed with us. 'We're like little orphans. Grandma and Grandpa wouldn't let us live up here, at the top of the house, like prisoners in the tower.'

'No,' Ruth said. 'They always had time for us. Remember how Grandma and Grandpa used to come into our room in the night to make sure we were OK? But Mother and Father are different. They have to work, they need their sleep; they don't have time to sit up and reassure us at night.'

'And they don't like me sleeping with the light on,' Joshua said, 'even though they know I'm scared of the dark. I hate this house. It's so cold, and the smell of the paraffin heater makes me sick. I want to go home.'

'Hush, hush,' I said, 'or you'll wake Mother and Father.'

'Do you remember how Grandma used to tell us duppy stories?' Ruth asked. 'And we'd be so scared we'd fall asleep under that patchwork quilt in no time. It used to be so cold in the country at nights. I loved that patchwork quilt. These blankets are rough and itchy.'

'Mm.' I stroked the rough blanket.

We always slept with the curtains open to let in the light. It was dark in our room. I longed for those tropical nights: moonshine, stars, dogs barking, cattle lowing.

'Do you remember how we used to love looking at the sky at night?' I said. 'We had a beautiful sky in Jamaica.'

'I used to love counting the stars at dusk,' Ruth said.

Joshua was the first out of bed. He stared at the black sky, saying, 'It's impossible to count the stars.'

We agreed. There were thousands of stars twinkling high above the world. We stood at the window reciting:

Twinkle, twinkle, little star,
How I wonder what you are!
Up above the world so high
Like a diamond in the sky ...

'Just like old times.' Joshua yawned. 'If only Grandpa were here now; he used to carry me back to bed, saying: "Early to bed, and early to rise, makes a man healthy, wealthy and wise." '

'Grandpa was so kind and patient.'

'Yes.' I helped Joshua into bed. He was fast asleep in minutes. We were homesick. We longed for the warmth of our grandparents' bodies, the times we used to climb into bed with them, especially on the night of the storm. We had come a long way, expecting to see replicas of our grandparents. Ruth began to snore. I drifted off to sleep thinking of Great-Aunt Minnie, the strange dream. I knew that if we were to settle in England we had to put the past behind us. But the past hung over our heads like a blanket of stars, it came out at night to haunt us; it refused to go away.

3

Suffer the Little Children

St Willliam's consisted of two schools, situated on opposite sides of the road. The old building dated back to the Victorian era; it was built near a railway station in a cobbled courtyard called 'Cloisters'. The chapel was in the courtyard too. You could hear the trains rattling past as you prayed in chapel on a Friday afternoon. There was a winding staircase going up, up, till you reached the attic for needlework.

The modern building was on the opposite side of the road. Morning assembly was held here in the hall. There was a well-equipped science laboratory and an airy library which housed classic literature and pictures of saints; there was a poster of Sir Thomas More. The caption said: 'A man for all seasons.'

Battersea Dogs' Home was a trot away from the school. So was Battersea Power Station, and there was a police station near by. The policemen in their navy uniforms complemented our bottle-green uniforms; two armies upholding the law, even if they were different laws.

It was assembly time. Sister Bernadette stood on the platform, pursing her lips. She had earlier inspected uniforms, told a few of the older girls to lengthen hemlines. Now she said, 'Hands up those who took communion yesterday?'

Every hand shot up except mine. I couldn't take communion until I'd been baptised into the Catholic faith. I felt like a sinner. Everyone looked at me. Sister Bernadette understood and nodded to me. Notices were read out. There was singing:

Lord for tomorrow and its need I do not pray,
Just keep me, guide me, love me, Lord,
  Only for today . . .

Sister Bernadette led us into reciting 'Hail Mary, full of grace, the Lord is with thee; blessed art thou among women, and blessed is the fruit of thy womb, Jesus . . .'

Then Sister Martha led us into the Apostles' Creed: 'I believe in God, the Father almighty, Maker of heaven and earth . . . I believe in the holy Catholic church . . .'

Finally the assembly ended. Sister Bernadette said, 'May I remind the younger girls: no running in the corridors, no giggling in class; don't fidget at your desks, it distracts your peers. You may go now: single file, please.'

'Yes, Sister Bernadette.' We left the hall.

The first lesson was English. A pale-looking nun with thin blue-tinged lips walked into the room, Sister Julie, our form teacher. There were several old-fashioned radiators hissing in the classroom. I stared because I did not know what they were then. There were pictures on the wall, even one of a black man kneeling in prayer. The caption read: 'Lord, teach us how to pray'.

'Good morning, girls,' Sister Julie said. There were notes being passed around, giggling. 'I expect you've all met Hope Byfield. Let's give her a big welcome.'

'Welcome to St William's, Hope.'

I felt like a goldfish in a bowl, on display.

'Girls,' Sister Julie said. 'Open your books. Today we'll be reading a passage from *Robinson Crusoe* by Daniel Defoe. Have you heard of Robinson Crusoe, Hope?'

'Yes, Sister Julie,' I said. ''E was shipwrecked on a deserted island. Then 'e found a slave called Friday . . .'

Everyone giggled. I wanted to hide my face.

Sister Julie said seriously, 'If you want to master the English language, Hope, you must pronounce your aitches.'

I always pronounced my aitches back home but I was so nervous. I was making silly mistakes. My classmates kept sniggering, especially when Sister Julie asked me to read a poem. In my eagerness to read and get it over and done with quickly, I mispronounced the words. I read, 'Daffodils' by William Wordsworth:

I wandered lonely as a cloud
That floats on 'igh o'er vales and 'ills,
When all at once I saw a crowd,
A 'ost, of golden daffodils . . .

There was a peal of laughter.

Sister Julie said, 'That's enough, girls. Thank you, Hope. You may sit down.'

I must have pulled my chair back too far when I stood up, and as I sat down I felt myself falling.

'Lisa James,' Sister Julie said, 'come here at once!'

'But I didn't do anything,' she protested, strolling up front, smiling. I noticed that the heels of her brown lace-up shoes had been walked down and her socks were drooping round her ankles. She had cropped brown hair and mean-looking grey eyes. She stood there biting her bottom lip.

'What sort of reception is this?' Sister Julie demanded. 'Laughing at someone else's misfortunes. Shame on you.'

'Sorry, Sister Julie,' she said. 'I'm sorry.'

'Go and sit down,' she said. 'Any more interruptions and you are all for detention tonight.'

I knew I had made enemies when Lisa gave me a dirty look. Then she passed a note to a girl called Grace, who wore her ginger hair in a ponytail with a fringe. She kept blowing the fringe upwards and shaking her ponytail from side to side. She reminded me of a horse. She read the note, passed it to a girl called Imelda. She was skinny with bushy eyebrows; she had a pageboy hairstyle. She chewed her hair as she read.

The next lesson was Geography. I hated that lesson. A small nun called Sister Agnes was in charge. She unrolled a piece of canvas and clipped it to the blackboard. Then she put some slides on a projector at the back of the room. She said, 'Does anyone know where Biafra is?'

'Somewhere in Timbuktu,' a girl called Avril said.

'Not quite,' Sister Agnes said. She was the smallest adult I had ever seen: stumpy arms and legs. Back home we would have called her a down-grown. She had long eyelashes and big brown eyes. She smiled. 'Timbuktu is the capital of Chad. Biafra is in Nigeria. They are both in Africa.'

Africa! The land of my ancestors. I was certain Great-Aunt Minnie and Uncle Isaiah's spirits had returned to the ancestral land. My heart swelled.

'We in the West are fortunate to have fertile land, enough food, water and wealth.' Sister Agnes operated the projector. 'We must help those who are less fortunate. That is why we send missionaries to Africa: there is a war in Biafra; people are dying of starvation, especially the little children.'

How could Grandpa be proud to be descended from Africans? What happened to the proud tribes? There before my eyes were pot-bellied children, walking skeletons and nursing mothers. I prayed Great-Aunt Minnie and Uncle Isaiah's spirits were at peace elsewhere. Africa seemed to be a land of misery.

'We must pray for those people,' Sister Agnes said. 'They need grains to plant; they need to be educated . . .'

There were hundreds of skinny women with bare breasts feeding babies with huge heads. There were flies everywhere. Old men walked with the aid of walking sticks, wrapped in rags. I wanted to hide my face. I was the only black girl in the class and everyone looked at me.

'Are people starving in Jamaica, too?' someone

29

asked. 'Is that why all those Jamaicans keep coming . . .'

Sister Agnes smiled. 'Jamaica is in the West Indies. The people from the West Indies were invited here after the war; we needed workers to make up for all the young men who died in the war, but now they are sending for their families . . .'

I felt awkward. I didn't belong in England. Why did my parents have to come to England? We were better off in Jamaica. I felt proud of my ancestors then. Now I wanted nothing to do with Africans. How could Great-Aunt Minnie have wished for her spirit to go back to Africa!

It was a relief when Sister Agnes switched off the projector and began to explain about soil erosion and drought. Soon the bell rang, announcing playtime.

The playground provided no refuge. There were no trees, no salt stones glistening in the distance, no friendly faces, just concrete. I recalled my cousin Robin saying to me in the schoolyard back home how he feared walking the length of an asphalted playground in England alone. That was precisely what happened to me on my first day.

Sister Helen was what I called 'a carbolic person'. She smelled of carbolic soap. She had blue eyes, a turned-up nose and missing ears, tucked under her veil. She had assigned three girls to look after me: Maeve, Mary and Sally. I could tell they didn't want me tagging along. They talked about what they did over the weekend: going to the pictures, ice-skating and the comics they were reading: *Tammy, Bunty* and *Jackie*.

'Have you got comics where you come from?' Maeve, a freckly-faced, dark-haired girl chewed her nails. I said no; she was appalled. 'You've never heard of *Tammy*, *Bunty* and *Jackie*! Where have you been living?'

Sally had long brown hair parted down the centre. She sucked the sleeve of her bottle-green jumper, saying, 'Do you watch *Tarzan*? My dad says coloured people come from Africa; they like swinging through the trees like Tarzan.'

Mary was a curly blonde. She had green eyes and a milky complexion. She said, 'My dad works with coloured people at Decca – he makes televisions. He says coloured people bring their food to work in flasks: rice 'n' peas and curried chicken, Sunday leftovers; yuk! He hates the smell of curry, and they talk funny. He wants us to emigrate to Australia. There are no coloured people there.'

'Yes there are,' Sally said. 'The aborigines are black.'

'Well, they don't really count, do they?' Mary said.

Once again I felt like an outsider. I had thought Precious and her friends were awful when I first went to school in the country back home but these girls were worse. They made me feel small, even though I was one of the tallest in the class. I didn't want to be their friend. Not that they wanted to be mine. They walked ahead of me whispering. I lingered, thinking: I'm an outsider, a foreigner.

Sister Helen patrolled the schoolyard, shouting: 'Don't throw litter, no standing around; get moving, girls.'

31

'Oi, Maeve, I want a word with you.' Lisa appeared. 'You stole my fountain pen and I want it back, you little toe-rag!'

'Who says I took your ink pen? You're a liar!'

'Imelda said you went into the classroom before assembly. And you stole Grace's pencil case last term. You're a thief.'

'Who're you calling a thief?'

'I want my fountain pen back.'

'Buzz off. I never took your rotten pen.'

'Yes you did, liar.'

'Right! I'm gonna get you!' Maeve pulled Lisa's hair.

'Ouch!' Lisa spun round, hair wrapped round Maeve's hand. Her fists flew. 'Get off me, you big bully.'

Shins were kicked, thumps sounded. A crowd gathered.

'Break it up.' Sister Helen yanked them apart. 'You'll be hearing from Sister Bernadette later on. The rest of you: move it, get going.' The crowd scattered.

'What are you looking at?' Maeve's red face snarled at me. Her friends kept tossing me snidey looks. Anyone would have thought the assault was my fault.

'No-nothing.' I was so nervous, I stuttered and my words rushed out in a jumble. 'No-nothing.'

'Get lost; we don't want you around.'

The last lesson of the day was PE. I fared no better. The nun in the bottle-green tracksuit was called Sister Philippa. She was pear-shaped. She helped me over the wooden horse, saying, 'Practice makes perfect. You need to practise.'

'Let her try the monkey bars, Sister,' Lisa said. Her friends giggled. I didn't understand why they found this funny until Lisa began to ape around.

Sister Bernadette was crossing the hall. She stopped and said, 'Lisa James, I will not tolerate such behaviour. Go to my office; same goes for you Maeve Martin.'

'Yes, Sister Bernadette,' their voices quaked.

'Carry on.' Sister Bernadette marched off like a soldier going to do battle.

Now I understood why Mother was in awe of Sister Bernadette. She could reduce a bully to a trembling jellyfish.

The lesson ended and everyone rushed off to the changing room. Sister Philippa came round, made sure everyone had showered. She felt hair and backs. 'Good.' She marched off.

'Do you have PE in Jamaica?' Avril asked. She was sitting on the bench next to me, taking off her white plimsolls. She wore wire-rimmed glasses. Her light-brown hair was held with an elastic band. She said, 'I never shower after PE. I just put my head under the shower. That's all. But make sure you're naked, just in case Sister Philippa comes back. Go on.' She sounded friendly.

'OK,' I said. The bullies were busy comparing tiny breasts, recalling the nursing women in Biafra. They ignored me, giggling. But I did not mind; I had found a friend. I slipped off my yellow sports blouse, my green culottes and the rest of my things.

33

I wrapped my towel around me and put my head under the shower briefly.

Avril took charge of me. 'Dry your hair, then we'll walk back to class together.'

For the first time in four weeks I wore a genuine smile, I felt happy. Someone wanted to be my friend. At home time, we walked to the bus stop together. How nice it was to have someone to confide in. Avril asked about my school in Jamaica. She said she'd never had a black friend before. I said I'd never had a white friend before. Avril had been to an independent school where she had learned calligraphy. When her father lost his job he couldn't pay the school fees, so she was sent to the convent school. She found it difficult to make friends; they thought she was stuck-up.

Lisa and her friends walked behind us. Maeve and her gang walked ahead. I couldn't work out which was worse: Lisa's gang or Maeve's posse. The hairs on the back of my neck stood up. I sensed something was wrong. I was soon to understand what was in the note Lisa had passed to her friends in class.

'Oi, you two!' a voice came from behind.

We kept walking. I heard a throaty cough. Someone spat. Still we kept walking. Maeve and her gang slowed down. They were pushing and shoving each other, giggling. We passed them.

'Wotcha, Hope,' Sally said. 'What's that on your hat?'

'I think someone spat on you.' Avril's face was flushed. 'I can't believe anyone could be so disgusting.'

I took off my hat to a peal of laughter. There was phlegm stuck to it. My heart swelled, tears welled up.

'Don't cry,' Avril said. 'Here, let me clean it off.' She took out a white handkerchief and cleaned my hat. God had sent her to my rescue that day.

'We'd better not take the bus,' Avril said. 'Let's walk home. They'll only embarrass you further at the bus stop.'

I felt powerless. Then I recalled the Bible story of Elisha in the book of 2 Kings 2: 23–24, how when Elisha went to Bethel: 'There came forth little children of the city, and mocked him, and said unto him, "Go up, thou bald head ..."' Elisha cursed them in the name of the Lord. 'And there came forth two she-bears out of the wood, and tare forty and two children of them ...' I prayed a similar fate might befall my enemies. But we were in the city; my prayers went unanswered.

We passed blocks of council flats, rundown mansions on the opposite side of the road.

'Don't look now,' Avril said. 'Here comes the coloured girls from Battersea County School.'

Sure enough, a group of black girls approached the bus stop, laughing at the tops of their voices. Maeve and Lisa had been ordered by Sister Bernadette to make up. Now both girls and their friends walked shoulder to shoulder with me.

'She thinks she's white.' One of the black girls glared at me. 'Look at her; coconut. She thinks she's better than us ...'

The bus came and the girls from Battersea County pushed and shoved.

'Get outa of the way you lot,' the black girls snarled. 'Don't let that coconut head get on before us . . .'

Maeve and the others drew back; they scorned the black girls who boarded the bus first, glaring at us. Lisa and Maeve's gangs came next. Avril and I sat upstairs trembling.

The conductor, a black man, rang the bell. 'Me noh want no trouble dis evenin'. No fightin' or fare dodgin'.'

The black girls cut their eyes on the conductor and sucked their teeth, fumbling in their pockets. 'Cho, man!'

'I hate this time of the day.' Avril took out her pass. 'Let's walk tomorrow. We'll walk along Queenstown Road, but we'll have to walk fast to avoid the Lavender Hill girls. The coloured girls there are as bad as this lot.'

'Yes, let's walk tomorrow.'

That night I tossed and turned in bed, waking Ruth. Joshua soon came into our room. He'd had a bad dream. But at least he hadn't wet his bed. I told them what had happened at school. They were surprised. They'd had a good day at their new school: everyone had welcomed them with open arms. They had walked home with the children on our street who also went to the local Catholic Infants/Junior school. They were going to call for them in the morning, too. They were the lucky ones.

Ruth cuddled me. 'You'll soon make friends.'

I sighed and said, 'Let's hope so.'

I drifted off to sleep, thinking: I can't wait to

leave school. I had come to England to get an education and become a writer, but the children at school were so beastly. My head was full of worries. I couldn't think about the future; getting an education was the least of my worries, let alone becoming a writer. All I wanted was to escape. I was vexed with Great-Aunt Minnie, talking about me going far in life and shining like a star; why did she have to place such a burden on my head?

4

Give Me the Old Time Religion

Dear Grandma,

Jehova guided us over the ocean safely. I hope these few lines will find you and Grandpa in the best of health. Mother and Father are well. Little Naomi has a chesty cough at the moment. Mother says it's caused by air pollution. Our house is so cold we have a fire going all the time. There's a gas fire in the sitting-room and paraffin – like kerosene oil – heaters in the bedrooms. We hate the smell of paraffin. It lingers on our clothes.

There is so much to tell you, Grandma, but I don't know where to begin. First of all, we miss you and Grandpa badly. We miss your smiling faces and your reassuring words. We try to love Mother and Father, but we can't help comparing them to you and Grandpa. We want to come home, but we know it is impossible. We must get our education before we can come home. We are afraid of upsetting Mother and Father. What if they sent us back home! It would be a disgrace. Everyone would say we threw away the opportunity of a better life It is such a burden trying to hold on to opportunity.

How's Dominic and her brood? Say hello to them. How's Uncle Ely and Aunt Esme? Say howdy-do for me. Tell them Joshua says he hopes they are taking good care of his kitten, Archie. Tell them I haven't seen Robin as yet. He lives far away, in a different part of the country. Father knows his address. I'm going to write to him. Give Aunt Enid my love. Ruth and Joshua send love, too.

Anyway, Grandma, England is not too bad: we have running water and electricity. We use them sparingly. Father says we must think of the people who have to go to the river or the public tank and do without the comforts we take for granted.

Joshua and Ruth have settled into their new school. They are very happy, especially Ruth. She sleeps well, eats well and she sings just like you, Grandma. When we are sad and lonely at night, we huddle together in bed singing until we fall asleep.

Sometimes Joshua has bad dreams. He's not allowed to wake Mother and Father; they work very hard. Father works for the local council, in an office. He says most black people over here work on the buses as conductors, or in factories, or they are ticket collectors for British Rail. Father says it's a good job he had a decent start back home. When he went for the job they couldn't believe it when he passed the aptitude tests. He works with a lot of stuffy old men. He hates it but he says you have to put up with a lot in this country.

Mother is a typist for an American firm. When she first came to England and went to the employment office, she told them she used to work in a post office back home. They sent her for a job as a cleaner. The woman who interviewed her used to be a missionary in Africa. When she found out Mother's history, she told her to take the cleaning job and go to evening classes, doing office practice and typing. Mother felt degraded but she took the job. When she passed the Pitman Shorthand examination, she got a job with the same firm as a typist. Some of the women refuse to talk to her. They still see her as a cleaner. Mother is unhappy in her work, but she says she has to stay because we need the money.

Mother and Father are a rarity over here. They are not bruising up their hands in a factory. There's something called class over here, Grandma. Father has warned us not to mix with people who are not in our class. At first Joshua said 'I can't ignore the children in my class.' Father said, 'I'm not talking about school, Joshua. I'm talking about people who have no etiquette.'

Please don't write and tell Father what I've said, Grandma. He will be very cross, so will Mother. They feel we must live up to the standard we were used to back home. That means not mixing with quashies, shouting in public, picking up cockney slang and playing on the street.

I must go now, Grandma. I can hear Mother coming up the stairs. She is going into Joshua's bedroom. Thank God he didn't wet the bed last night. God bless and keep you and Grandpa till I hear from you again. Write soon.

Your same,
Hope.

'Are you allowed to play out?' Three boys knocked at our door. They were dressed in cowboy outfits with black hats. Each held a toy gun. 'We're playing soldiers and Red Indians.' They fired their guns at Joshua: 'Pow, pow, pow . . .'

'Joshua,' Mother called, 'how many times have I told you not to open the front door? Who's there?'

Mother was in the kitchen feeding Naomi. The kitchen consisted of a gas cooker, a wooden table in the centre, a grocery cabinet, a fridge and a white (heavy-duty) sink. There was linoleum on the floor. Mother sat at the dining-table with Naomi on her lap, pursing her lips. Her dark face was smooth and she wore lipstick and Cutex. She spooned mashed vegetables into the baby's mouth.

'Can I play out front with my friends, Mother?' Joshua ran into the kitchen. 'Please, Mother.'

Mother preferred us to play in the garden. But the garden was so small you couldn't run the length at full speed without bashing into the wall. Mother had also planted cabbages and carrots. The vegetables were unhealthy-looking. There was a barren apple tree. The grass was patchy. When we first arrived we couldn't believe people had such tiny gardens.

'Not today,' Mother said. 'Besides, you know how your father and I feel about you playing out front.'

'It's not fair,' Joshua said. 'I want to play out.'

'You do enough playing at school,' Mother said. 'Go and tell your friends you can't play out.'

Joshua slunk off. He had made friends with the boys on our street. They all went to the same school. He was happy. At the same time he was unhappy because he wanted to fit in, so he needed a cowboy outfit. The boys also swopped comics.

41

He began to ask for pocket money. Father said there was no extra money to spare. We'd cleaned them out. Our fares took all the money they had, not to mention household bills. Now they were trying to replenish the emergency kitty.

'Can I go ice-skating with Emma and Chris, please, Mother? Emma says her mum will be taking us by car,' Ruth said. 'They're coming to collect me at noon.'

Mother said, 'Tomorrow is Sunday. You've got catechism in an hour's time. Then you've got confession with Father Joseph, followed by choir practice.

Ruth said, 'Why do I have to become a Catholic? And why do I have to pray to Mary; why can't I pray directly to Jesus?'

'You are not praying to Mary; you're only asking her to intercede for you . . .' Mother said seriously. 'Anyway, your Father and I want you to be good Catholics; we also want you to get a good education, so that you can get good professions! Go to your room and stop questioning me.'

'Oh! It's not fair.' Ruth went running up the stairs.

'I'll have to discipline that child,' Mother said. 'It seems your grandparents have spoiled her . . .'

I was vexed; I cut my eyes on Mother. Grandma and Grandpa hadn't spoiled us, not really.

'Who's a good girl?' Mother said, spooning food into Naomi's mouth. 'I hope you're not giving me bad-eye, Hope?'

'No, Mother,' I lied. 'Can I ask you a question?'

'What is it now?' she snapped. 'You children

are always asking questions. Have you learnt the Apostles' Creed?'

'Yes, Mother.' The question stuck in my throat.

'Good. Father Joseph will be pleased,' she said. 'Your father and I promised to bring you children up as good Catholics. Now go and ask Mrs Parsons if she will baby-sit Naomi while I take you children to church. And make sure Joshua does up his tie properly.'

Mrs Parsons was a war widow. She lived next door. Her house was cold and smelled of burnt coal from her fire. She had no pets, said they were too expensive to keep. She played the piano whenever we visited. She never went to church, didn't believe in God. Mrs Parsons said people went to church out of habit. If there was a God he wouldn't have allowed so many young men, including her Andrew, to die in the First World War. All her relatives were dead, except for a nephew who had emigrated to New Zealand.

I was taken aback when I first saw Mrs Parsons. I had never seen an elderly white lady before, let alone had tea with one. She was so thin. Still she had smiling clear blue eyes and she was stylish. She wore her long grey hair in a bun. She watched old movies on TV and read library books. She went to the library once a week. When I asked why she went so often and owned very few books, she said: 'My dear, if I had a shelf full of musty books, I'd never have a social life. I go to the library for warmth and conversation.'

Mother liked Mrs Parsons, who wore dainty old shoes with buckles. She also wore a hairy-looking animal around her neck (her stole) and sometimes she wore a mangy fur coat. She wore gloves whenever she went out. She would call over the fence to Mother: 'Yoo-hoo, Beatrice; the kettle is on the boil.'

She always made a pot of tea. She said tea bags were too modern for her, and she was fond of cucumber sandwiches. Once I made the mistake of saying 'kokomber sandwiches'. She said: 'No, no, my dear; you say cucumber sandwiches.' I was embarrassed. We always said 'kokomber' back home. Father had said he liked Mrs Parsons the moment she spoke. She was in his league.

Mrs Parsons offered to become six-month-old Naomi's childminder. (Her first childminder had ill-treated her.) She had nothing to do all day, except for reading her books and watching *Peyton Place*, an American soap opera. Mrs Parsons insisted my parents called her Bunty.

'Don't just stand there looking into space, Hope,' Mother said. 'Go and give Mrs Parsons the message and hurry back.'

St Luke's was an old church. It was situated in front of a big common. It was dark and cold. The light fought its way through the stained glass windows. There was a font filled with holy water in one corner. There was a table at the back where the parishioners put their letters, cards, to each other. There were narrow steps leading up to a balcony where the choir looked down on the congregation. In a dark corner tapering candles burned and flickered. The smell of incense filled the air. There were numerous pews, and no one had a special place; very few people greeted each other before or after the service. It was so different from our Baptist church at home.

It was Saturday morning. Mother dropped us off at church and went home. I was cross with Mother because she'd snapped at me. She didn't want to know what was troubling me. Ruth and Joshua were annoyed, too. They wanted to be with their friends. Instead they had to spend Saturday morning in the church hall, learning to be good Catholics. After catechism we had to go into the confession box in church, sit behind a dark curtain, knowing Father Joseph was on opposite side. We hated the thought of confessing everything. We felt guilty when we saw the elderly priest afterwards.

Father Joseph was a tall, pale-looking man. His eyebrows were bushy and met in the middle of his forehead. He always wore a blank expression.

'Forgive me, Father,' I said. 'I have sinned against my parents: I love my grandparents better than them and I want to go home. I know my parents have spent a lot of money on my air fare and I should be grateful but I can't help it. I think bad thoughts, mostly about the children at school. They are always teasing me. Oh, Father, forgive me . . .'

Father Joseph was silent for a long time. He coughed and said, 'Bless you, my child . . . As penance, you should light a candle and say five Hail Marys . . .'

'Thank you, Father.' I left the box. My next task was to go off to the dark corner, drop some money in a wooden box, take a candle, light it, then say: 'Hail Mary, full of grace, the Lord is with thee . . .'

Mother had told Father Joseph that Ruth and I could sing. It wasn't long before we were members of the choir.

That Sunday we climbed the winding stairs and joined the children in the choir. They smiled at us. Our parents sat below with Naomi and Joshua. Mother wore a hat and gloves. She liked wearing gloves. Father wore a dark suit. There were altogether four black families in the congregation. Everyone stared at us. I had never noticed my colour until I came to England. Lord, Lord, I prayed, why am I different? Why do you allow people to stare at us so?

Notices were read out: births, deaths, anniversaries, forthcoming weddings; new members were named and welcomed. We were considered old hats. We'd been members for almost two months. It was a family service. Father Joseph said, 'We come together as a family and begin our worship with a prayer:

'*I confess to God Almighty*
And to you my brothers and sisters
That I have sinned . . .'

The congregation stood in reverence; their voices rose to heaven. Instead of joining in the confession, I prayed for my grandparents, the parishioners and the animals on the farm at home. I wanted to be back in church, standing next to Grandpa, listening to the pastor praying, Grandma singing in the choir.

46

I wanted to see familiar faces, hear Grandpa's old horse Gideon neighing in the churchyard. I wanted Toby to come sniffing down the aisle, looking for Grandpa. I wanted my old life back. Instead I found myself singing:

Kyrie eleison, Kyrie eleison
  Kyrie, eleison.
Christe eleison, Christe eleison . . .

Ruth and I lifted our voices, along with the other children. How strange: now we were singing in Latin. We understood the Latin words. Father Joseph had seen to it. We practised at the vicarage one evening a week. Our life was filled with Catholic activities: church and school.

Sanctus, Sanctus, Sanctus.
Dominus Deus Sabbaoth . . .

Ruth's voice rang out. She shifted on her feet, hands shaking as we shared a songsheet. She wore a red coat with black buttons. She wore a black hat and black boots. We still couldn't get used to wearing boots. They hurt our ankles. I wore a grey coat and black hat, too. Joshua wore a dark suit; a miniature of Father. I had trouble keeping up with the others as they sang. Ruth was absorbed. We sang:

Benedictus qui venit in nomine Domini.
Hosanna in excelsis . . .

Father Joseph prayed for the people in Biafra. I cringed, feeling as though my blackness singled me out. I stared at the contented-looking white children. They sang heartily. Then it was time for the Apostles' Creed:

'I believe in God the Father almighty,
Maker of heaven and earth
And in Jesus Christ his only Son our Lord ...
I believe in the holy Catholic church ...

I believed in the Baptist church. I felt disloyal to the Catholic faith. I would say ten Hail Marys afterwards.

When the service ended, my parents shook Father Joseph's hand. He greeted them with a bland smile. 'The children have settled in nicely. I think it's time they were baptised.'

'Thank you, Father,' my parents said.

We were to be converted. There was no turning back; we had no say in the matter. I was afraid Father Joseph would tell my parents what I had said during confession. Instead he said, 'I expect to see you girls for choir practice Wednesday evening. I hope you enjoyed the service.'

'Yes, Father.' We lowered our heads.

Had we enjoyed the service? I certainly hadn't. Father Joseph couldn't preach like the pastor back home. He never thumped the pulpit. He prayed with a lack of passion and he shook hands limply. Nothing amusing ever happened in church, not unless you counted Father Joseph draining the communion cup after everyone else had finished. I looked at his bulbous nose, thinking, 'Give me the old time religion anytime.' What I needed was a good Baptist service to soothe my troubled mind.

5

If the Cap Fits

Dear Grandma,

Greetings to you and Grandpa. I'm a Catholic now. I was baptised in the school chapel last week. Afterwards Sister Bernadette, the headmistress, presented me with a rosary. I've been given a new name, after a saint, Cecilia.

Grandma, my chest is growing. When I take my clothes off in the changing room for PE (that's Physical Education, you play games: tennis, netball, hockey, rounders and lots more) everyone sniggers. They say I should be wearing a bra instead of a vest. Can you please send me a bra? My chest has grown overnight. I am getting hairs on my body, too. I don't like it. What does it all mean?

My life has turned upside down overnight, Grandma. One minute I was a little country girl, and now I am a city girl. I like England really. There are lots of places to see and beautiful shops: we went to a store called Army and Navy to buy our uniforms. I saw all manner of things. I never knew one shop could sell so many beautiful, expensive things.

We travelled on a train to a place called Victoria Station, Grandma. I was afraid the train would roll off the track; it didn't. There are so many people, trains, cars, buses and motor bikes in England. One of the girls at school asked me if we had double-decker buses in Jamaica. I said we had lots of them, I lied. I said five Hail Marys afterwards. I can't get used to praying to a lady.

Grandma, the children at school laugh whenever I speak. They say I have an accent. I didn't know I had an accent. I'm trying to change it. Sister Julie, my form teacher, is very tall and pale. Her lips are almost blue. She's got sugar, a diabetic. Sometimes she goes to the hospital for her blood sugar to be monitored. Last week I mispronounced a word. She said: "Hope, if you want to get on in this country, you must lose your accent and learn to pronounce your aitches." Now I'm afraid to speak up in case my accent lets me down.

England is a land of books, Grandma. There are libraries everywhere. You don't have to buy books if you don't want to. You can borrow them from your nearest library. Anyway, Sister Julie says I must read a lot. She has given all the girls in my class a little notebook. We have to write down the title of all the books we've read. She says at the end of term she will give a prize to the person who's read the most books. I'm reading a book called "The Diary of Anne Frank". It's about a Jewish girl called Anne Frank. She and her family hid from the Germans during the Second World War. It's a sad story.

Sometimes I feel persecuted like Anne. The children in my class keep touching my hair, exclaiming, "Ugh, it feels like cotton wool." I hate my hair for attracting attention, too. You used to say Ruth and I were lucky to have growing hair.

It's not growing as fast as it used to and it shrinks at the slightest hint of rain.

By the way, Grandma, one of the cho-chos I brought from home has begun to grow. I went into the cupboard to get something and there it was, sprouting in the dark. I put it in a plant pot with some earth. When the weather changes I'm going to plant it in the garden.

Grandma, we have a very nice neighbour. Her name is Mrs Parsons. She is very stoshus, like the high-colour people back home. She wears gloves and talks with her tongue between her teeth like Mr Trelawny. Ruth, Joshua and I feel comfortable with Mrs Parsons; maybe it's because she reminds us of the dainty old ladies in church at home. One thing that bothers me about Mrs Parsons: she never goes to church and she doesn't believe in God; she won't go to heaven when she dies, Grandma. It's such a shame.

Nothing more to say, Grandma. Give Grandpa and everybody my love. I close now with love. God bless you. Write soon.

Your same,
Hope.

'Ding, a ling, a ling; the school bell ring: knife an' fork a fight fe dumplin'.' I pretended I was in the schoolyard back home. We used to recite the rhyme whenever we heard the bell.

It was the week before Christmas and snow was expected. The school was decorated with tinsel, streamers, balloons. Sister Bernadette wasn't in a festive mood. Quite a few of the older girls were hitching up their skirts, loosening their ties and forgetting their hats, setting a bad example for the younger girls. Sister Bernadette inspected uniforms, and woe betide anyone who forgot their hat, wore the wrong coloured socks or tights. She gave detention as if it were going out of fashion. She demanded to know who went to communion on Sunday. If there wasn't a hall full of hands in the air, the guilty parties had to give an account. Right now the hall was full of hands pointing to heaven, which brought a smile to Sister Bernadette's face.

Sister Philippa, the PE teacher, was also the music teacher. She played the piano and the guitar. She stood up front, on the platform, ready to play.

Sister Bernadette said as Christians, it was our solemn duty to give thanks to God for keeping us safe throughout the night. The coming together for morning assembly gave everyone a chance to pray, especially those who had forgotten to do so when they woke up. Finally, we sinned in words and deeds daily; morning assembly was a good time to ask God's forgiveness, and to foster positive thoughts.

Sister Martha prayed for God's guidance throughout the day. She prayed for tolerance, peace and understanding.

Then Sister Philippa strummed the guitar. We sang 'New every morning is the love.'

Morning assembly ended. The first lesson of the day was Religious Education with Sister Agnes. We talked about free will, the difference between right and wrong. Sister Agnes told us the parable of the wise man and the foolish man: one man built his house upon the rock, the other built his house on the sand. She said, 'Now which was the wise and which was the foolish man?'

Sylvia was a brown-haired girl who wore braces. She had been to boarding school, and she stuttered, too. But she wasn't impeded by her stutter. 'The o-one who b-built his h-house upon the s-sand, Sister. He w-was a f-foolish man.'

'That's right,' Sister Agnes said. 'Can anyone name the seven sacraments?'

Maeve sucked her pullover sleeve, smiling. Mary chewed her nails. Sally giggled; they found Sylvia's stutter amusing. The rest of the class remained silent.

'Baptism, Confirmation . . .' Sister Agnes sighed. 'Can anyone explain the meaning of Original Sin . . .' She sat back waiting. There was no reply. 'Very well,' she said. 'Homework: I want everyone to explain the meaning of Original Sin, list the seven sacraments, followed by the meaning of Sin: mortal, grave, venial . . .'

The next lesson was French. Sister Julie was late.

'What was it like living in the bush, Byfield?' Lisa's face was dead serious. When I gave her a blank stare, she said, 'I bet you used to climb trees and all that, didn't you?'

I went to the loo, if only to escape for a few minutes.

'*Ferme la porte*, Byfield.' Lisa joked. 'Were you born in a barn or something?'

'*Oui*.' Maeve laughed. 'She was born in a barn.'

'*Non*,' Sally, the girl whose hair was parted down

the centre, said. 'She was born in a field: By-field, geddit?'

My face burned as they chorused: '*Oui, oui* . . .' I hated being the centre of attention, as much as I hated French. When I first joined the class, I was thrown in at the deep end with no extra help. I couldn't pronounce the words properly.

'Look, look,' Imelda shouted. 'It's snowing.'

Maeve and her friends rushed to the window, oohing and aahing. It was as if there were millions of tiny white feathers floating down from the sky.

'Have you ever seen snow, Byfield?' Grace asked.

I swallowed and said, 'No.' Then the bullies dragged me across the room, pushing my face towards the window pane. The snow settled on the window-sill like ice shavings.

'Hope has never seen snow . . .' They were aghast.

No one came to my rescue, not even my friend Avril. She kept her head down. The others laughed nervously, pleased the bullies were picking on someone else.

Sister Julie entered, clapped. 'Girls, girls; silence *s'il vous plait*. I'm sure you've all seen snow before . . .'

At lunch time we crowded into the dinner hall and lined up with our trays. There were roast potatoes, roast beef and peas, followed by sponge with pink icing on top and custard. I looked forward to school dinners. The food was appetising.

Of course, someone had to annoy me. We sat at long tables with lots of chairs. The nuns saw to it

55

that you seated yourself at the nearest table, not cluttering up the hall. Maeve and her gang sat on the same table as Avril and me. They kept flicking peas in my direction. A pea bounced off my nose. I choked on a potato and Sister Helen, the carbolic nun, who was on dinner duty, knocked my back until the potato slid down.

'There's plenty of food on your plate, Byfield,' she said. 'Take your time; there's always seconds.'

This remark brought a fit of giggles, nudges. I provided the comedy of the day.

'It's not my fault I choked, Sister,' I said. 'Someone fling a peas in my direction.'

'I think you meant someone "flung a pea" at you, Hope,' she said. 'Do try to speak properly.' She moved on.

'Do they use knives and forks at your old school?' came a voice. 'And what did you used to eat for lunch?'

After lunch the children went out to play. There were little groups all over the playground. Avril and I stood in the slushy snow, talking. Our hands were cold and we tucked them into our blazer pockets. Meantime Lisa and her friends stood near by, talking about pop stars: the Beatles and Cliff Richard were popular.

Lisa and Maeve used to be rivals. But now that there was a newcomer to boss about, they forgot their squabbles and concentrated on me. They got hold of a skipping rope, charged in my direction, mean faces intent on mischief.

'Whoops, you shouldn't get in the way, should you?'

I prayed for some evil to befall my enemies: break an arm or a leg perhaps. I wanted to fight back, really hurt the bullies. I felt a terrible rage boiling within but I was too nervous to retaliate. I rubbed my ankles where the skipping rope stung me.

'We'll be off to Australia by the summer,' blonde-haired Mary said. 'My dad's going to the Australian High Commission today.'

Sally whispered, 'My parents don't like coloured people; they've warned me not to get friendly with you-know-who.'

'My dad would go spare if he ever catches me talking to coloured people,' Maeve whispered.

'Her hair has gone all funny, hasn't it?' Lisa said.

'Your hair looks like cotton wool,' they said. 'What's the matter with it? It's gone all white.' They closed in on me, fingering my hair. 'Yuk! It feels horrible.'

'Get off,' I kept saying. 'Leave me alone . . .'

'The snow has settled on your hair, Hope.' Avril's hair hung limply. 'You'd better go into the loo and dry it.'

I went to the outside loos. When I saw my hair in the mirror I could have cried out; my hair was covered with snow. Why couldn't the snow have melted, like it did when it settled on everyone else's hair?

'Let's have a puff.' I heard Lisa's voice coming in my direction. I darted into a cubicle. She and the others came in. They were smoking. 'Who's on guard?' she said. 'Maeve, it's your turn.'

'I'm not standing around like a ninny,' she said. 'Someone else can do it. Gimme a puff.'

Caught you! I thought. I would tell Father Joseph when I went to confession on Saturday. Then I thought, why should I hide myself away? I'm doing no wrong. I came out. They said, 'Don't you dare tell anyone, Byfield!'

There were footsteps. Lisa dropped the cigarette at my feet and dashed into a cubicle. The others dashed into cubicles, slamming the doors and pulling the chains in the loo.

'Byfield?' Sister Martha came in. 'Why are you wasting time when the bell has gone? The others have gone inside.' She sniffed. 'Have you been smoking?'

'No, Sister Martha,' I said. 'It wasn't me.'

'Who's in there?' She sniffed. 'Sister Bernadette will have something to say about this . . .'

The bullies came out. They stared at me knowingly.

'Right,' Sister Martha said. 'What have you to say?'

'It wasn't us, Sister Martha,' Lisa said. 'Honestly. Cross my heart and hope to die.'

'I take it you are the culprit, Byfield?' Sister Martha turned. 'Speak up!'

'It wasn't me, Sister Martha,' I said. 'Honestly.'

'Go to your classroom!' Sister Martha said.

We walked out in single file, quietly. When we were nearing the classroom Lisa said, 'You didn't see us smoking, Byfield, did you? We'll get you if you tell anyone.'

The incident was forgotten. The next lesson was history. The bullies were model pupils, even smiling at me occasionally.

'Byfield,' Sister Martha marched into the classroom at the end of the day. 'Sister Bernadette would like to see you in her office. I suggest you sit and wait till the others have left the room; give yourself time to think . . .'

The bullies went off, throwing me menacing looks, as if to say, 'We'll be waiting at the bus stop.'

Sister Bernadette stood looking out of the window. The pigeons were safely tucked up under the railway bridge. Jesus suffered on the cross. I stared at the painting of Our Lady and child. Sister Bernadette patted the crucifix she wore.

'You wanted to see me, Sister Bernadette?' I spoke first.

'I see you've settled in nicely, Byfield,' she said. 'How do you find crossing the road to get to and from lessons?'

'It can be quite dangerous in the mornings,' I said. 'The drivers are all in a hurry. They don't seem to care about the pedestrians; they're impatient.'

'And do you feel that we are like that at St William's?'

'No, Sister Bernadette,' I said. 'Everyone is so . . .'

'So patient?' she said in an ironic tone.

I wasn't sure where the conversation was heading.

Sister Bernadette said, 'How are you settling in?'

I knew the bullies would have a go at me if I said anything. I couldn't bring myself to tell Sister Bernadette.

'Everything is fine, Sister Bernadette.'

'I hear you've made some new friends: smokers.

Sister Martha said she caught you and a bunch of girls in the loo . . . Would you like to talk about it?'

'It wasn't me, Sister Bernadette, honestly.'

'I see.' Sister Bernadette walked round the desk. Her habit made rustling noises. She said, 'Sister Agnes tells me you are an avid reader. She thinks you ought to spend more time in the library, less time in the playground with people who are liable to lead you astray.'

'I will, Sister Bernadette,' I said. 'May I go now?'

'You may go. And by the way, I will be sending letters home to all parents; I do not condone smoking.'

I thought I had been let off the hook that evening, especially when I discovered Lisa and her friends had gone home. I decided to walk along Queenstown Road, past the rundown three-storey houses with paint peeling off the doors. I wanted to save my bus fare to buy a Christmas present.

'Oi, hoity-toity?' A group of black girls approached. They were the Lavender Hill mob. They blocked my way, snatched my hat, passed it around, jeering. 'Posh uniform, eh!'

'Give it back.' I ran from one to the other. 'Give it back.' I was tripped up. My uniform was soiled. My satchel went flying. 'Leave me alone.'

One of the girls laughed. 'She thinks she's white.'

'No I don't!'

'If the cap fits wear it.' They tried on my hat. Their hair had been straightened. They had straight, shiny hair worn loose. They kicked my satchel around, kicked my hat, too. 'Let's undo her plaits.'

(My hair had shrunken because of the snow.) They taunted me. 'Where's your long silky hair . . .'

Adults passed by; they looked the other way. A few workers from the television factory near by strolled past. I picked up my satchel and hat and hurried off to the sound of laughter. I fought the tears, thought of the girls back home. They would have loved my hat; they took pride in their uniforms. They loved my hair, too: the thick plaits, the stiff ribbons. I used to be so proud of my hair.

In my hour of humiliation I cursed England. It was a hateful place. I wanted to lay down my burden, education, trample it under foot, for it was the root of my troubles. At that moment I saw a flock of pigeons flying towards the railway bridge, their home, sanctuary. How I envied those birds their wings. I wanted to fly away. Instead I made my way to Clapham Common, where I sat on the swings and passed the time away, staring into space, shivering in the cold, dreaming of home. Finally I reluctantly picked up my satchel and headed for Mrs Parsons' house; it was my job to collect Naomi.

Mrs Parsons was in the kitchen pressing flowers between a book. She closed the heavy book and set it down on the dining-table, saying: 'I'm afraid your mother has already collected Naomi.' She studied me, adding: 'Oh, dear, don't tell me you've been fighting?'

'It's the Lavender Hill mob,' I said. 'They like to pick on anyone who wears a different uniform. They were making fun of my hair.'

'You have lovely hair,' Mrs Parsons said. 'It's so soft and fluffy.'

61

'That's what the girls at school say; they're always making fun of my hair,' I said. 'I hate my hair.'

'Oh, you mustn't say that, my dear,' Mrs Parsons said. 'Believe me, you've got lovely hair. When I was very young my mother used to do my hair in ringlets. All the girls at school teased me. I spent hours in front of my dressing-table mirror desperately brushing out the curls, but my mother always put them back. She loved ringlets, said they made me look like a cherub. I've hated ringlets ever since. Anyway, in my experience people only mock others when they're jealous of them for one reason or another.'

I hated to say my hair would never arouse jealousy: it wasn't long and silky and it wasn't soft and curly. Instead I smiled and said, 'I suppose you're right.'

'Ah, you're wearing your best face,' Mrs Parsons said. 'How about a nice cup of tea and a buttered scone with lashings of jam before you go home?'

'Yes, please.' I loved Mrs Parsons' homemade scones. They were delicious.

'By the way,' Mrs Parsons said, 'I've got something for you. I picked it up at a jumble sale today: a book called *The Craft of Flower-Pressing*. I used to love pressing flowers when I was a girl. I'm sure it will come in useful; a nice hobby for those rainy days when you've got nothing to do.'

'Thank you,' I said. 'I can't wait to read it. My art teacher has got a book called *Flowercraft*. I like looking at the pressed flowers and ferns. Mother has got some old cork table mats that she's going to throw away. I think I'll press some pansies and daisies in a book. Then I'll glue them onto the mats, give them a face-lift.'

'Clever girl,' Mrs Parsons said. 'That's the spirit. Now, you sit yourself down while I put the kettle on.'

As I sat at the dining-table watching Mrs Parsons pouring loose tea into the teapot, I felt as though I were at home in Grandma's kitchen, watching her boiling bissy tea in the billy can. I imagined Mrs Parsons' features changing into those of Grandma's. I was content to just sit, browsing through my book as the kettle whistled a happy tune.

6

White Christmas

You couldn't take your troubles to Father, not like you could to Grandpa. Father was preoccupied with his own troubles. He hated his job and wanted to leave but he had applied for numerous jobs to no avail. He was frustrated by lack of opportunity. The employment agencies had no work to offer, that is, if a man didn't want to work on a building site, wear an overall, or a London Transport or a British Rail uniform.

Mother fared no better. She had made a rod for her back. By taking a job as a cleaner, then rising to become a typist in the same firm, she was regarded as the tea lady. Coffee cups were left lying around and she was frequently asked to go and buy the milk and make the tea. She wouldn't have minded if everyone took their turn. If work was slack, the supervisor would say: 'Oh, Beatrice, since you've got nothing to do, why don't you make yourself busy; be a love and make the tea. You don't mind, do you?'

My parents were not alone. Their friends fared no better. Father talked about the people in his 'league'. There was an actor, a singer, a dentist and a travel agent. They'd been friends from back home. They often attended functions at the Jamaica High Commission. These functions attracted people who wanted to move up in the world. Father and his friends never passed up an invitation.

The travel agent had whiskers and a moustache. His shop was cold and the posters of the West Indies, on the wall, were always falling down. The phone rarely rang; few would-be tourists entered the shop. He sat at his desk in a nice suit, warming his hands on the paraffin heater.

As for the actor, he had appeared in a few films, including *A High Wind in Jamaica* with some well-known stars, and he'd appeared on *Jackanory*. We were in awe of television: moving pictures on a screen was a miracle. And there was this medium-height, well-spoken man talking about his fears and hopes for the future. He wanted to shine like a star; he was tired of playing the understudy. He was certain his career would take off in Jamaica. He'd applied for a job as a disc jockey with one of the radio stations out there.

The singer had had a hit with a record about a train. He was tall and well-dressed. He wore a wide-brimmed hat and a handkerchief in the top pocket of his dark jacket always. He entertained us with folk songs.

The dentist was a sorry sight. He was tall and dark with cropped hair parted at the side. He had a private practice and he, too, spent a lot of time waiting for patients to walk through the door. Whenever he got a black patient, they would gripe about the bill and expect him not to charge them. After all, he was one of them. If they were back home, they would have brought him a goat, chicken or a pig. Here, they couldn't afford dental bills. The dentist wanted to go home, but he'd left Jamaica with high hopes. He couldn't go home until he'd achieved something. Father's friends were single. A wife and children would lower their standards. But despite their problems, they were always good company. We children were looking forward to seeing them on Christmas Eve.

The snow threatened to keep people prisoners in their homes. It climbed up the front door, covered the gardens and the roof tops. Chimneys belched smoke and occasionally a cat sat on the roofs. The children in our street made a snowman on the pavement. The cold seeped into our bones and we refused to leave the house. There were snow fights and a lot of laughing in the street. The rag-and-bone man came round; his horses were dragged down by the snow and the weight of the cart.

'Cold enough for you lot?' He stared at us. We stood at the front door watching the children playing in the street.

Mrs Nosey Parker nodded to the rag-and-bone man. 'Serves them right if they're cold; they'd be better off in their own country. Before you know it Battersea will be overrun . . .'

'Too right.' The rag-and-bone man reined in the horses.

Mrs Nosey Parker was never without her sponge rollers. She said: 'Wot's that you've got there, mister? I could do with a settee. My one is on its last legs.'

'Gimme ten bob.' He unloaded the sofa and carried it across the road. 'It's in good nick.'

'Five bob,' Mrs Nosey Parker said. 'It ain't worth a shilling more.' They went indoors with the settee.

'Let's make a snowman.' Joshua turned to Ruth. 'We'll ask Mother for an old scarf and a carrot.'

'Yes. Just like the ones on the Christmas cards.'

A few days before Christmas Father bought a Christmas tree. There was a sense of excitement through the house. We'd never seen a real Christmas tree before. We helped Mother to decorate it with baubles, red satin bows, Christmas lights, a fairy on top of the tree. What made Christmas really special was the parcel we received from our grandparents. Mother opened it but stopped when the brown paper gave way to Christmas paper. There was a Christmas card, too. Mother put the lone card on the coffee table; the present went under the tree.

Christmas Eve, we went shopping in a local department store called Arding and Hobbs. Father Christmas sat outside the glass door with his sack and bell on the ground, looking cross: a group of children had pulled his beard; he sat adjusting it.

That evening Father sat on the sofa dusting his LPs. Mother was preparing rum punch in the kitchen. Meantime Mrs Parsons kept her company. She'd brought over hot mince pies. We'd never seen mince pies before. We said, 'They're not at all like patties.'

Mrs Parsons said, 'There's mixed fruits inside.'

'Times like now I wish I was back home,' Father sighed. 'I miss the Christmas festivities: Jonkonnu, Christmas market, going to church on Christmas

Sunday, visiting relatives, the smell of sorrel wine. I even miss the smell of the farm . . .'

'I know how you feel, Jasper.' Mother carried the punch bowl into the sitting-room, placing it on the coffee table. 'I can't wait for spring: the flowers and leaves on the trees.'

'Why can't we go home now?' Joshua asked.

'Because I gave up a good job, came here thinking life was better. Now I don't have the means to go home.'

'Well I don't want to go home, not yet,' Ruth said: 'not when there are so many toys and pretty things in the shops.'

'No more talk of home,' Mother said when there came a knock at the door. 'Fix your faces. Our visitors are here.'

What a surprise we children got! These visitors were not expected: a group of people all wrapped up in thick coats, scarves, boots, etc. They composed themselves and sang, 'We wish you a Merry Christmas.'

'Merry Christmas to you, too.' Father gave them some money and they went away.

'Christmas is a magical time for children,' Mrs Parsons said. 'My mother used to decorate the banister with holly berries and ivy. There would be mistletoe hanging at the door and candles on the Christmas tree. We had a holly wreath hanging outside the front door. Father used to sit in an arm chair reading the Christmas story: "And he sent them to Bethlehem, and said, 'Go and search diligently for the young child; and when ye have found him, bring me word again, that I may come and worship him also.' " Afterwards we ate hot mince pies round the log fire. We went to midnight mass, too. . . .'

The door knocked; this time Father's friends arrived. They kept saying, 'Rum punch and mince pies? I ask you. Haven't you got any brandy, Jasper?'

Brandy was served.

'I fancy some music; calypso.' Father put an LP on the turntable. We children watched the record going round and round on the turntable. The adults sang 'Jamaica Farewell'.

The sing-song ended and the travel agent said, 'Guess me this riddle and perhaps not: One piece of white yam serves the whole world. What is it?'

The men shouted, 'The moon.'

The actor said, 'Anancy story, I'm going to tell an anancy story.' He changed his voice, slipping into patois. 'Once upon a time, Brer Anancy was passin' dis likkle 'ouse. Dere was a beautiful girl sittin' at de window an' 'im fall in love wid 'er. Next day 'im pass de 'ouse again. De pretty girl was still sittin' at de window. 'Er maddah was hangin' out de washin', some pretty frocks. Brer Anancy transform 'imself into a man. 'Im seh, "Marnin', Miss Lady. Me love yuh daughter an' me wahn fe marry 'er." ' De ooman said. "Go weh fram me gate, sah. No man good enough fe me daughter."

'Next day Anancy stop at de gate. De pretty girl still sittin' ad de window. 'Im say, "Marnin, Miss

Lady. Me love yuh daughter an' me wahn marry 'er."

De maddah said, "Go weh fram me, sah. Yuh cahn 'ave me daughter's 'and in marriage unless yuh can guess 'er name."

'Each day Brer Anancy pass de 'ouse. De girl lock up indoors. He said to de maddah, "Is yuh daughter name Adlyn; is yuh daughter name Dimples; is yuh daughter name Hilda?"

'Of course, Anancy was wrong. 'Im decide to enlist de 'elp of green lizard. Lizard was cunnin'. 'Im crawl 'pon 'im belly all ober de place. 'Im 'ear 'tory odder peeple never 'ear. Dem ignore lizard, say 'im cahn understan' labrish . . .

'Lizard said: "Aaright, Brer 'Nancy. A gwine find out 'er name fe yuh, but yuh haffe giv' me a reward."

' "Yeah, man," Brer Anancy said. "Yuh find out 'er name an' me will giv' yuh a reward, Lizard."

'So lizard hide eena de bush an' wait. De maddah said, "Lawd me tired, sah. Me haffe do all dis washin' sake o' me daughter. But me not complainin' 'cause me love 'er to death."

'Lizard decided to mess up de washin' on de line. 'Im crawl eena mud an' den crawl ober de washin' pon line. When de maddah come fe tek up de washin', she bawl out, "Anybody see me trial! Smaddy dutty up Rosalee's pretty frock dem?"

' "Aieee!" Lizard crawl off. 'Im meet Brer Anancy 'pon de way. 'Im seh, "Brer 'Nancy, me find out 'er name. But yuh haffe gimme de reward first."

' "Cho, Lizard," Brer Anancy said. "Yuh know

seh me will look after yuh. Just tell me de name noh, Lizard."

'Lizard seh, "She name Rosalee. Now gimme me reward."

'Brer Anancy pick a stick. 'Im whack Lizard ober 'im back: twack, twack, twack! Lizard run eena de bush as fast as 'im could. Brer Anancy laugh: "Kya, kya . . ." Dat's 'ow green lizard get de stripe down 'im back.'

We children knew a different version of the Anancy and Lizard story, but we didn't have the heart to say so; we laughed just the same. In fact, everyone laughed, even Mrs Parsons. She said, 'I don't believe in violence, but this Brer Anancy is certainly cunning.'

'Music!' the singer said. 'How about some music?' He belted out 'Mule Train . . .' His voice was really powerful. He rushed off into another song. Ruth began to dance.

'Gwane, pickney gal.' The dentist surprised us. He never ever spoke in patois. 'Drop two foot!' He crooked his arms, bent his knees and danced. 'Do de funky chicken, du-du-dum . . .'

Before long everyone joined in, crooking their arms, dancing and singing: 'Do de funky chicken, du-du-dum . . .'

Mrs Parsons said, 'I hate to break up the party, folks, but it's midnight.'

'Happy Christmas!'

'Shouldn't we have gone to midnight mass?' Ruth asked.

'The church is so cold, I'm sure Father Joseph

and baby Jesus will forgive us this one.' Father closed the subject.

I would have liked to have gone but I sensed that Father preferred the warmth of home and the company of good friends.

Christmas morning we woke to see stockings at the foot of our bed and a large present wrapped in silver paper. Ruth and I examined our red and white felt stockings, squeezed them.

Ruth opened a present wrapped in silver paper. It was the parcel from Jamaica. 'But what is this?' She stared at flat pieces of wood and a sheet of paper with instructions for Father. Then she added, 'Grandpa has made a doll's house for me. Oh Grandpa, Grandpa. A doll's house.'

I eagerly opened a smaller packet. 'I don't believe it! Grandpa has carved Dominic and her chicks . . .'

'Hope, Ruth!' Joshua came running up the stairs. 'Grandpa has carved Gideon and Toby for me. Oh, Grandpa . . .'

Our stockings contained wool, knitting needles, biros, books and crayons. After a while we looked out of the bedroom window. The garden was so white with snow it hurt our eyes.

'Good morning, children,' our parents said as we entered the kitchen. The scent of fried plantains, ackee and saltfish greeted us. We showed off the toys from Grandma and Grandpa.

'You can open the presents under the tree after lunch.'

We were impatient. We begged and begged. Mother gave in: Ruth got a big talking doll. It kept saying, 'My name is Anne . . .' I got my very first wristwatch. Joshua got a cowboy outfit and a toy gun. He went around, shooting: 'Pow, pow, pow . . .' Father's friends, who'd left long after we'd gone to bed, had given us money. We felt really special.

'Our first Christmas as a family,' Mother said. 'Sit down and grace the table, Hope.'

I recited: 'For health and strength and daily bread, we praise Thy name, amen.'

'Amen.'

'Where's Naomi? We've brought her a present: a suda.'

Father laughed. 'They call it a dummy over here. Are you children trying to tell us something?'

'She never stops crying these days,' Joshua said. 'You and Mother are always fussing over her.'

Father said, 'We fuss over all you children, Joshua. We love you all. Naomi is asleep; she's teething, that's all.'

Ruth went into the hallway. She opened the cupboard door. She returned. 'This is for you, from us.'

Our parents were full of cheer. 'Real flowers, thank you, children. I wish we could afford them all the time.'

'You children are something.' Father studied my face. 'Where did you get the money from?'

'I saved my bus fare and walked to and from school.'

'We can't let you do that, Hope,' Mother said. 'Though I must say it was very thoughtful of you. From now on you children will get a shilling a week each, pocket money.'

73

'Thank you, Mum and Dad. That's the best Christmas present ever . . .' We kissed our parents, feeling truly happy.

We went to church on Christmas Sunday. Father Joseph read the sermon from sheets of paper. (At home the pastor memorised everything.) Finally he and his helpers fed the congregation and gave them wine. The congregation sang:

Hark! the herald angels sing,
"Glory to the new-born King . . ."

I recalled Grandpa telling me to enjoy our 'green, sunny Christmas and leave white Christmas to the future.' Father's voice rang out, singing, 'Hark! the herald angels sing . . .' For a split second I wished Grandpa was standing next to me. Then Father looked down and winked at me. I looked up at him and smiled, thinking, you sound just like Grandpa. There was a feeling of acceptance. Thoughts of Grandpa were stored away for now. I held Father's hand tightly, for I really wanted to get to know him better.

7
English Heritage

Dear Grandma,

I received your letter and was glad to hear from you. I am pleased Dominic has had another set of chicks. The farm must be overrun with them. Beware of the hawks and mongooses! Remember what happened to Frizzel?

We children are pleased to hear that Grandpa's got another dog to keep Toby company. Rover is a lovely name for a dog. We miss not having any pets. Our garden is tiny so we can't have pets. Father won't allow animals in the house. We keep talking about Toby and old Gideon.

I forgot to tell you about Christmas: thank you for the lovely presents. We'll always treasure them. We had a lovely time. Mother invited our neighbour, Mrs Parsons, over on Christmas Eve; she didn't want her to see the Christmas in alone. Father's friends came, too. They entertained us with riddles, anancy story, music and dancing. It was fun.

England is a strange place, Grandma. You can't just drop in on friends or relatives on a Sunday afternoon, like we used to. You have to make appointments. We are still waiting for Robin and his parents to visit us. They were supposed to spend Christmas Day with us, but the snow blocked the motorway, made driving impossible.

75

Mother said I should never have written and asked you for a bra. She said I should have asked her. But I'm pleased you wrote and told her. I'm wearing a bra now.

Grandma, some of the schoolgirls in England are worse than the girls back home. They are always picking on me. Sometimes when I'm angry I slip into patois and the children at school laugh at me. I feel foolish when it happens. I'm trying to change my accent, sound like a real English schoolgirl. Otherwise the children will keep teasing me.

Joshua and Ruth send their love for you and Grandpa. They've settled in school. We miss you and Grandpa very much. When we are sad and lonely at night we sing. Ruth sounds just like you, Grandma. We sing in the choir at church. I can't sing the high notes, unlike Ruth.

It's Friday evening over here. I have to help Mother with the shopping. You should see the food stalls in the market along the Northcote Road; I've never seen so many fruits and vegetables in one place. You should see the laundry, too. We have machines to wash our clothes. Mother puts our dirty clothes in laundry bags in the week. Father drops Mother and me off at the laundry on Friday evenings, after we've put the shopping away. I feel sorry for the women back home, washing all those clothes by hand.

Must close now, Grandma. I have to go shopping with mother. I close with love. Write soon.

Your same,
Hope.

There was excitement throughout the school, caused by the opening of a tuckshop. Sister Martha, the deputy head, who often stood guard at the schoolgate, was concerned about the number of girls sneaking out of the playground at break, to buy sweets at the local corner shop: a tuckshop would put a stop to their antics.

Sister Agnes was in charge of the tuckshop. She nominated two girls to run the shop. They were in my class: Amy and Venetia. Amy had thick brown hair tied back. Venetia had long blonde hair worn with a simple headband. They were top of the class and best friends. Venetia's father was Italian, her mother was English. Amy and Venetia came from well-off families. Both girls were picked up by their mothers after school in expensive cars. The other girls were envious, especially those who had to make their own way home.

Amy and Venetia never ever spoke to me. I watched them secretly always. I imitated the way they spoke, watched the way they carried themselves, tossed their head back. They talked about going to Guides, piano lessons, swimming, the theatre on Saturday mornings, going to ballet . . . I dreamed of doing all those things.

'Can I have a Mars bar?' I asked.

Amy handed me the chocolate. 'Here you are. And in future you ought to say: "May I have a Mars bar, please?" '

I cut my eyes on her, took the change and walked away.

What I disliked about these girls was the way they stared at my chest in the changing room after

PE. They wore vests tucked into their knickers. I, too, wore a vest but it wasn't tucked into my knickers.

'Snobs,' Avril said as we walked out into the playground. 'Just because their mothers drive Mercedes, they think they're better than us. My father used to have a Jaguar; he sold it when he was made redundant. Now we've got a Vauxhall Viva. I hate being poor: I've had to give up my dancing and music lessons.' She added. 'Here comes you know who?'

'Lend us sixpence, Byfield.' Maeve approached me.

'Yeah,' green-eyed Mary said. 'Lend us a tanner.'

'I haven't got any money.' I walked off, holding my chocolate protectively.

'Oi, thingy-bob,' freckly-faced Maeve said. 'Don't walk away from us. Who do you think you are?'

'Empty your pockets,' long-haired Sally said. 'Go on.'

'Get off.' I struggled, kicked, when rough hands pinned me to the wall. Spiteful-looking faces leered at me, fingers poked my body; my pockets were emptied: nothing.

'Don't you just love winding her up.' They took my Mars bar and went away laughing. 'Who shall we pick on next?'

I had been looking forward to eating my chocolate; now my mouth had a bitter taste.

'Do you go to bal-let?' I turned to Avril, who stood there looking helpless. I hid my feelings behind conversation.

'Of course.' She sounded really surprised. 'You don't say "bal-let"; ninny. You say ballet, sounds like bal-eh.'

I felt foolish. Why couldn't I have kept my mouth shut?

'Don't take it personally. I'm only trying to help you.'

'It's all right. I don't mind, really,' I lied.

The bell rang and playtime was over. The next lesson was Art. The art teacher, Mrs O'Casey, was medium height and she had cropped hair, rather like Twiggy. She wore a brown eye-shadow and black eyeliner. She showed me how to use the pottery wheel, and I made a vase. Mrs O'Casey promised to glaze it in the furnace. She was really pleased with it, so I felt really good for once.

The lesson progressed. I experimented with colours. Mrs O'Casey said there was an exhibition at the National Gallery and she and Sister Agnes would be taking a group of us. A letter would be sent to our parents, asking for permission and a donation towards transport.

Mrs O'Casey said, 'Art is for everyone. It is better to see the real thing hanging in a gallery, than to look at pictures. Get your parents to take you round art galleries, study a few pictures, especially those that have been painted by famous artists: Matisse, Manet, Picasso, Van Gogh.'

I felt ignorant when a dark-haired girl called Louise said, 'My father prefers David Hockney, Miss.'

Mrs O'Casey said: 'Of course, there are those

who prefer the contemporary painters. Personally I prefer the old masters: Renoir, Monet.'

'Are there any coloured painters, Miss?' Lisa asked.

The word 'coloured' drew attention to me again; there was this thing about colour. I shrank into the top of my uniform.

Mrs O'Casey said, 'I believe there was a coloured American painter called Horace Pippin. He painted a picture called *The Domino Players* – a coloured family at home in the kitchen, playing Dominoes. It's rather like Matisse's *The Painter's Family*; he painted his family at home playing draughts.'

'Oh.' Lisa seemed disappointed.

Horace Pippin caused a surge of pride within me. Black people were artistic after all. I thought of Grandpa, he'd carved Columbus's ships for the pastor, carved our Christmas presents, too. I thought of the villagers. They played dominoes all the time. There was an art to playing dominoes. I wanted to say: 'Please, Miss, my grandpa is artistic . . .'

That evening I handed Father the letter about the outing. He was reading a book called *The Lonely Londoners* by Sam Selvon, a Trinidadian writer. He put the book aside and tore the envelope open as we children and Mother sat in the sitting-room, watching *Coronation Street*. There was this old woman wearing a hairnet, just like the old ladies back home. She was called Ena Sharples and her friend was called Minnie. I thought of Great-Aunt Minnie then.

'Art appreciation?' Father said. 'Better than the

last letter: smoking in a Catholic school! I thought the children were well-disciplined. Choose your friends carefully, Hope.'

Mother said sternly, 'I don't want you mixing with the wrong people, Hope. Don't let anyone lead you astray.'

Father said, 'I'm beginning to wonder if I've chosen the right school.' He added, 'We really can't afford to send you on this trip, Hope. We've just paid all our bills . . .'

'Oh.' I stared at the television, Ena Sharples was quarrelsome. 'It's not fair. Everyone will be going!'

'All right,' Father said. 'But it will have to come out of the money your mother and I have put away for an emergency.'

'Make sure you put it back, Jasper,' Mother said.

'It's all right, Father,' I said. 'I don't want to go, not if it means having the electricity cut off.'

'Of course I'll put it back,' Father said. 'It's not everyday your daughter gets a chance to go to an art gallery.'

'Thank you, Father.' I could have hugged him.

The day of the school outing came and Avril was absent. She was in hospital, having her appendix out. The girls paired up as we joined the coach.

Yoko was a Japanese girl. She was big-boned and wore glasses. She had joined the class in the new term. The bullies kept pulling their eyes at the corners, giggling. I felt sorry for Yoko and tried to befriend her. She didn't like being around me. But I noticed she kept hanging around Antonia and Jane. The strange thing was: they ignored me, but they befriended Yoko. She bought them lemon

81

bon-bons from the tuckshop, followed them round the playground.

'Hurry up, girls,' Sister Agnes said. 'Yoko, since you haven't got a partner, why don't you sit next to Hope?'

She did, but she froze me out. Her uniform smelled of stale cooking. She was reading *Oliver Twist*. I opened *Jane Eyre*. Not a word passed between us.

Sister Agnes sat up front. Mrs O'Casey sat at the back. The coach moved off. We drove past Battersea Power Station, where the chimneys puffed out smoke, soiling the blue sky with dirty grey patches.

'Battersea Power Station supplies the electricity we use,' Sister Agnes said. 'One of London's best known landmarks.'

We passed Battersea Bridge. My first glimpse of the River Thames. I put *Jane Eyre* in my satchel. It was high tide and there was a river patrol boat speeding through the murky water.

'Westminster,' the driver said. 'We're approaching the Houses of Parliament, and Westminster Abbey is on your left.'

'English heritage,' Mrs O'Casey said. 'The Houses of Parliament, Westminster Abbey, Poets' Corner: Charles Dickens and Robert Browning are buried there.'

'Whitehall.' Sister Agnes informed us as we crossed Parliament Square. 'The heart of the country's government . . .'

'Sir Winston Churchill.' The driver pointed to a statue. 'Downing Street's coming up. That's where the Prime Minister, Harold Wilson lives; the Chancellor of the Exchequer is at Number Eleven.'

'St James's Park and Buckingham Palace coming up,' Sister Agnes said. 'There's a memorial to Queen Victoria in front of the palace.' She hummed: 'I vow to Thee my country . . .'

'We're approaching Trafalgar Square,' the driver said. 'Look: four lions guarding Admiral Lord Nelson.' He pointed. 'Trafalgar Square was built to commemorate his victory at the Battle of Trafalgar in 1805.'

Finally we reached our destination.

'Single file, girls, please,' Sister Agnes said.

The coach stopped outside the National Gallery; two magnificent columns looked down on Trafalgar Square. We left the coach; I had a feeling of not belonging because I had no companion. I made my way to Sister Agnes's side.

We toured the gallery, quietly admiring the paintings. Some of the famous names Mrs O'Casey talked about were there: Rubens, Rembrandt, Constable, Turner . . . I walked behind Sister Agnes thinking of the past: there were so many artistic children back home. They would never have the equipment to paint, let alone see all those beautiful paintings.

Soon Sister Agnes said it was time for lunch. We left the gallery and crowded into the coach. Later we went to see the pigeons in Trafalgar Square. There were hundreds of them scrambling in the snow, perching on the tourists' shoulders, sitting on their arms as they fed them. Icicles hung from the fountains. The tourists shivered, spoke in foreign tongues, reminding me of the Bible story about the tower of Babel.

Sister Agnes went round, saying: 'Be careful of the pigeons, girls; they're fond of soiling people's clothes.'

A pigeon flew overhead. I ducked. It fouled my hat and I rummaged through my satchel, trying to find a tissue.

Mrs O'Casey handed me one. 'Pigeons!'

Meantime Yoko, Antonia and Jane stood near by, giggling. They threw coins in one of the fountains, reciting: 'Three coins in the fountain; which one will the fountain bless?'

I would have liked to have thrown a coin in the fountain but I had no spare coin. There was a sense of relief as Sister Agnes gathered the flock.

The following week, during the art lesson, Mrs O'Casey pinned several photographs on the wall, including one of Westminster Abbey, the Houses of Parliament.

'Your vase is on the table over there, Hope,' Mrs O'Casey said. 'Not bad for your first attempt.' She patted my shoulder. 'I do like that vase.'

'Thank you, Miss.' Only a parched land which thirsted for water could have understood what that compliment meant to me.

'Hark at clever clogs.' Maeve picked up my vase as Mrs O'Casey's back disappeared out the door.

Lisa gave Maeve a knowing look. 'Nice vase, isn't it?'

The volcano within me rumbled when something crashed to the floor. My vase broke, scattered.

'Whoops,' Maeve said. 'I'm ever so sorry.'

'Pick it up, you – you . . .' My face burned with rage.

'What a cheek! Who does she think she is?' Lisa tatted.

'Are you gonna make me?' Maeve demanded.

I snarled, 'If you don't pick it up, I'm going to–to . . .'

'You're going to what? Lisa shouted. 'Teacher's pet!'

'What's going on in here?' Mrs O'Casey returned.

'Nothing, Miss.' Maeve glared at me as if to say, 'If you grass, I'll sort you out after school.'

Mrs O'Casey looked from Maeve to Lisa. They toyed with clay. She looked at me. I fiddled with a paintbrush. The other girls lowered their heads, kneading clay, operating pottery wheels or experimenting with colours.

'Who broke this vase?' Mrs O'Casey picked up the pieces.

'It was an accident, miss,' Maeve said.

'I see.' Mrs O'Casey looked at me. 'Is that so, Hope?'

'Yes, miss.' I trembled with rage. I hated my school: why had I come to England? Why did Cousin Archie and Aunt Jemima give me those treasures, make me promise to get a good education? I fought tears as the questions swam round in my head. Then I recalled a dream I'd had the night before in which Great-Aunt Minnie told me, 'Smile, child. Better must come one day.' At that moment I was too angry to smile.

At playtime I was left to skip alone. Avril was at home now, recovering from her operation. Yoko trailed after Antonia and Jane, carrying a skipping rope. All of a sudden there was a tug and pull on my skipping rope.

'Oi, Byfield,' Maeve said. 'I'm gonna get you.' She tried to take my skipping rope, wrestled with me.

'Go on, Maeve.' Cropped-haired Linda and her friends came running. 'Bash the little ratbag, go on!'

As always I attracted attention: a crowd appeared. Maeve elbowed me in the ribs. Pent up anger exploded: I lunged at her, twisted the offending limb behind her back.

'Ouch!' she screamed. 'You're hurting me.'

There was a look of surprise on her friends' faces. They shouted, 'Let go of her, you little toe-rag!'

Hidden strength surfaced. 'Not until she says sorry.'

'You must be joking,' Maeve cried.

I gritted my teeth and twisted her arm. Maeve kicked at my shin. Her friends hurled abuse at me. I released the arm and pushed Maeve forward when I saw Sister Julie approaching.

'What's going on?' Sister Julie was on playground duty. Her lips were almost white. 'I asked a question.'

'Nothing, Sister,' Maeve said. 'I fell over and hurt my wrist. Hope was helping me. I'm all right now.'

'Good,' Sister Julie blew the whistle. 'Get moving!'

The crowd broke up. We lined up in single file: the girls who'd been victims of the bullies, before I came along, peeped down the line at me in admiration, smiling; one or two of them gave me the thumbs up sign in recognition of my victory. For the first time since I'd come to England, I felt as though I truly belonged. I walked on air back to my classroom, reciting in my head, 'Better must come one day.'

8

Lord of the Dance

Needlework was a lesson which brought a flood of nostalgia. I thought of Great-Uncle Lincoln: the time when Grandma took Robin and me to visit him; how he pedalled that sewing machine. I daydreamed about Grandma taking Robin and me on a journey: how we slid down the hill on our bottoms, the aeroplane flying overhead. Then I recalled the silver bird flying over the blue Caribbean Sea. It took away my childhood.

'As I was saying last week,' Sister Joan, a pale-skinned nun with white eyelashes, said, 'whoever makes the best Easter bonnet will be the winner. The competition will be judged in the assembly hall; the winner will receive an Easter egg.'

Needlework lessons were taken in an attic in the old building. Sister Joan went from table to table, showing us how to lay out patterns. There were boxes containing patterns, felt, lace, ribbons, pins, fabrics. But we'd also brought in our own materials: straw hats, denim material, coloured tissue paper, artificial flowers, ribbons.

'I'm making a bonnet with lots of flowers round the brim,' Avril, who was fully recovered from her operation, announced.

'What I'm looking for is originality,' Sister Joan said.

I had cut out a large denim-blue circle. I was stitching a casing round the brim, ready to thread through with elastic. I was making a floppy hat.

Everyone was excited about the competition. Sister Joan examined the work, praised the girls and said, 'In the old days ladies used to dress up in fine bonnets and gloves and parade in Battersea Park on Easter Monday. Who knows, if your bonnets are good enough, you could wear them to this year's Easter Parade.'

Finally we labelled our work and put it in cardboard boxes with our names on. Then we left the needlework room, crossed the road. Our next lesson was House Craft.

'We're making hot cross buns today,' Mrs Redomski said. She'd come to England as a Polish refugee. Her hair was swept up in a bun. She wore thick-rimmed glasses and a poncho.

'Please, miss,' Maeve said. 'I'd like to make an Easter egg. I don't like hot cross buns.'

'I'm afraid we're all making hot cross buns today.' Mrs Redomski addressed the class. 'Have you all brought in your money for the ingredients and your baking tins?'

'Yes, miss.' We went up in single file as Mrs Redomski called our names. Afterwards we washed our hands, some of the girls tied their hair back with elastic bands; then we put on aprons and got out the cooking utensils.

We made hot cross buns, put the cross on top to signify the crucifixion. We washed up the utensils, put them away.

'Yuk!' Lisa managed to get chocolate on her

hand, half a Mars bar which she'd bought at the tuckshop. She took it out of her skirt pocket. 'I was saving this for later. It's melted; it's so warm in here. Look at my hand! It's filthy; I look like a chocolate-coloured kid.'

'Ah, ah, ah.' Came the response from her friends.

I never knew when the subject of colour would surface. But I anticipated it, gritted my teeth whenever it came.

Mrs Redomski said, 'I see we have a comedian in our midst. I don't think that's funny. Go and wash your hands.'

'Sorry, miss.' She washed her hands in the sink.

The bell rang. We cleared up and hurried off to the art room where Mrs O'Casey wore bell-bottom trousers and a smock top. She was so skinny she had earned the nickname Twiggy.

'Nothing brings out the best in an individual like a competition.' Mrs O'Casey had put out glue, scissors, paper, paint. We brought along the other bits and pieces that were needed: pressed flowers, linen material, sea stones, etc.

'Originality is the key,' Mrs O'Casey said when dark-haired Louise produced three hard-boiled eggs and proceeded to paint faces on them.

'I'm going to make a Mary Quant shoulder bag with a daisy on it.' Maeve was busy sketching. 'My mum likes her designs.'

'So do I,' Mrs O'Casey said. 'The only problem is: you're going to need a sewing machine to stitch the seams and the motif; we haven't got one in the art room. I would rather you didn't take the material out of this room.' She thought, then said, 'I suppose Sister Joan could keep an eye on you.'

'Thank you, miss.' Maeve beamed.

Mrs O'Casey stopped at my table. 'What are you making, Hope? Looks very interesting.'

'I'm making a paper weight, miss.' I varnished a large sea stone which Mrs Parsons had given me. The idea came from her book on flower-craft.

'That's very original,' Mrs O'Casey said. 'I love the idea of decorating a stone with pressed daisies. But I wouldn't use any glue; the varnish alone will hold the daisies in place. Keep up the good work.'

'Teacher's pet.' Lisa hissed.

Mrs O'Casey examined Amy's book mark: pressed flowers and covering film were glued on to a piece of pastel-blue ribbon. 'Well done.' Mrs O'Casey moved on.

Venetia was making a linen cushion cover. She embroidered daffodils, tulips and blue bells on to the fabric. Mrs O'Casey stopped. 'Very original, Venetia.'

Avril made greetings cards using lilac-coloured textured paper: she cut the paper into shape, outlined the insets with a black marker, then she glued pressed flowers on to the paper.

'I can see I'm going to have a hard time judging this competition,' Mrs O'Casey said.

The bell rang. We cleared up, ready to cross the road, enter the cobbled courtyard once again; this time we were going to mass. It was the Friday before Easter. Father Joseph was the school chaplain. He liked punctuality. Nevertheless, some of the girls strolled into the chapel and seated themselves, gossiping: Maeve said she knew who the winner would be; Mrs O'Casey was a fan of Mary Quant. Everyone was in a competitive mood; they cared little about mass. Very few people heeded Father Joseph's words. He talked about the meaning of Easter: Jesus was crucified on Good Friday, on the third day He rose from the dead; Christians celebrate the resurrection on Easter Sunday. Sister Philippa strummed the guitar. We sang 'Lord of the Dance.'

On the last day of term the competitions were judged after morning assembly: in our year group Yoko had made a bird's nest on top of her bonnet. There were tiny chocolate eggs in golden wrappers and yellow chicks walking round the brim of the hat. It should have taken first prize, but someone had splashed ink all over the bonnet.

Antonia won the competition: she had decorated the brim of her straw hat with edible daffodils which her mother had made with icing sugar. She accepted her Easter egg from Sister Bernadette, wearing the coveted bonnet.

My bonnet had been stolen. I was angry with God; he must have been sleeping when the theft occurred?

Sister Joan had said: 'I can't understand it; we've never had vandalism and theft before. It can't be one of my girls.'

Venetia's linen cushion won the art competition. She accepted a large Easter egg. I joined her on the platform, accepting the runner up prize.

'Well done, Byfield.' Sister Bernadette handed me a medium-sized Easter egg.

'Thank you, Sister.' I accepted the consolation prize. Envy reared its head: a few of the girls in the hall cut their eyes on me. I felt so proud; nothing could spoil my day.

Sister Bernadette said, 'Byfield has only been with us a short time and already she's made a contribution to our school. Let's give her and Venetia a big hand, girls.'

At home time Maeve and her friends caught up with Avril and me along the road. 'Mrs O'Casey gave you-know-who a consolation prize because she likes her; teacher's pet.'

'Ignore them,' Avril said. 'They're dead jealous, especially Maeve. She thought her Mary Quant handbag was a winner. I bet Lisa ruined Yoko's bonnet and Maeve stole yours. After all, she was allowed to make her handbag in the needlework room. You should have mentioned it to Sister Joan.'

'No,' I said. 'Sister Joan wouldn't believe me.'

'She thinks everyone is a saint,' Avril said. 'Let's take the bus tonight. I want to get home early. Mother and I are going Easter shopping.'

Mother and Father came home carrying parcels. They were going to a function at the Jamaica High Commission. Father's friends were going, too. Mother had bought a white dress with black spots and pink neck and sleeve bands.

'Second prize, eh?' Father said. 'Not bad at all. Let's hope you excel in all your other subjects.'

'Oh, Jasper,' Mother said. 'Give her time to get used to the school.' Then she added, 'I wonder where I've put my straightening comb?' She tried on a pair of sling-back shoes. 'The girls at work are mad about Ossie Clarke designs.'

'I thought you didn't get on with the girls?'

Mother smiled. 'Half of them are pregnant; a change has come over them. I wish it could be like that all the time.'

'Work is over now,' Father said. 'Drop the subject.'

'Who's going to look after us?' Joshua asked.

'Bunty has offered to babysit,' Father said.

'Mother, can you straighten my hair, please?' I asked.

'No,' she said firmly.

Naomi was crawling all over the place, pulling at the coffee table: Mother had crocheted a sort of centre-piece with peacocks round the rim. The vase of artificial flowers sat on it. Naomi reached up, pulling at one of the peacocks.

'We'll have to get her a playpen,' Mother said. 'She's all over the place, pulling everything down.'

'We can't afford, it,' Father said. 'This dinner and dance is quite expensive, not to mention our shopping spree.'

'We've been a bit reckless,' Mother said. 'But we deserve it. We haven't been out, got dressed up for ages.'

On Good Friday we children watched the crucifixion on TV: *King of Kings*. We wept as Jesus carried the cross up the wooden steps, wearing a crown of thorns. The cross fell on top of Him and we winced. We sobbed when He was crucified. We knew the story of the crucifixion by heart. To see it on television was a miracle.

'It's only a film, children,' Father said. 'Honestly, you children believe everything you see on television.'

Easter Saturday we watched our parents dressed to go out. Mother had straightened her hair and wore it loose. She looked pretty in her spotted dress. We loved to watch her dress. Ruth and I took turns, walking round in Mother's sling-back shoes and gloves, giggling.

Joshua polished Father's shoes, tried them on, singing, 'You can't to to heaven with a number nine shoes . . .'

'I can.' Father fastened his bow-tie, buttoned up his dark jacket. 'Behave yourselves for Bunty, children. She's a godsend. And make sure Naomi doesn't wreck the place.'

'Your shoes are as shiny as a dollar piece, Father.' Joshua tied the shoelaces.

'I feel like a lord tonight.' Father braced his chest.

'And you look really stylish, Mother,' Ruth said. 'Can you straighten my hair like yours?'

'You girls have good quality hair,' Mother said. 'You should be proud of it. Why, many girls would love to have the head of hair you have.'

'Straight hair is pretty.' Ruth took up her doll, pulled the cord in its back. It kept repeating, 'My name is Anne . . .' Ruth added, 'I just want to look pretty like my friends.'

I recalled Ruth asking Grandma if she could have a new uniform so she could look like her friends at school. How easy life would have been if all it took was a uniform to fit in. Now you needed silky hair and a milky complexion.

95

'Let's not spoil the evening,' Father said. 'I'm in a dancing mood. We'll discuss this matter another time. Let's get going, Bea. I've got the boys' tickets.'

'Honestly, you and your boys.' Mother applied lipstick.

I was beginning to understand Father: being treated like an office boy wasn't easy to digest, and he was getting good at filling in application forms; he couldn't stomach the rejections. The only time he felt like a real man was when he was dressed up, attending a function where he could dance the night away, forget his troubles. The strain of not belonging was crucifying his spirit, and there was nothing I could do about it, except work hard at school to make him proud of me.

9

The Doll's House

Rain was a thing we children loved when we were very young: the pitter patter of raindrops on the roof, the branches of the coconut trees wilting under the weight of the rain; the orange and coffee blossoms being beaten down by the rain; the parched earth quenching its thirst, the earthy smell. The banana leaves trembled, the grass glistened. The animals lowed, grunted, cackled as the rainwater soaked their dwellings. The hot asphalted roads popped their bubbles, cooled down. We children often played in the rain, turned our faces skyward, tried to drink the warm rainwater.

In England raindrops spelled trouble. Watching the rain from our bedroom window was best of all. But to be in the rain in the schoolyard was to invite ridicule: my hair got wet, rainwater sat on it, made it shrink. Then someone would say, 'Your hair looks funny, ah, ah, ah.'

Thereafter I pleaded with Mother to straighten my hair. Everybody had straight hair; the rain merely made it limp. I would have preferred limp hair rather than shrunken hair. I thought if I had straight hair I would fit in. As the rain beat down on the roof, Ruth and I stood over the gas cooker in the kitchen, two forks on the burners.

'Make sure the forks are really hot,' she said.

'That way my hair will be dead straight; I want pretty hair.'

'Don't worry,' I said. 'Your hair is soft anyway. You only need a warm fork to straighten it.'

'Hurry up,' Ruth said. 'Mother will be back soon.'

It was Saturday morning. Mother had taken Joshua and Naomi shopping for new shoes. Father and the boys had braved the rain, gone to the Oval to watch cricket. Back home, he and his friends always went to Sabina Park in Kingston to watch cricket. Mrs Parsons had gone to the library so there was no one to look after us. Mother didn't like taking all four of us shopping. She said Naomi was a handful, let alone another three children moaning and groaning.

There was a smell of singed hair I used the fork as a hot comb, straightening Ruth's hair.

'Open the back door,' I said. 'And close the front door. We don't want the smell escaping into the hallway.'

It wasn't long before I'd managed to run through Ruth's hair. She had brought her tortoise-shell handled mirror from home. She now had a matching hairbrush. She brushed the hair, saying, 'At last my hair is soft and pretty.'

The thought never occurred to us that Mother would notice the difference.

'Your turn.' Ruth shook her head, hair moving. 'Hurry. Your hair will take longer. You know how tough it is.' Ruth held the mirror while I straightened the front of my hair, made a fringe. I was impatient to have beautiful hair.

'What's going on?' Mother opened the door, sniffing.

'We just wanted straight hair, Mother,' Ruth said. 'We want our hair to look like yours.'

'I have a mind to give you a good hiding,' Mother snapped.

'Straight hair is nicer than crinkly hair!' Ruth cried. 'That's what all the girls at school say.'

Mother was holding Naomi, whom we secretly resented. She was the loved child; we were the intruders.

'Go to your room at once.' Mother's hair was wet, water dripped down her face. 'Wait till your father gets home.'

'If he beats me I'm going to run away!' Ruth said.

'Come here, young lady.' Mother stormed into the hallway, stood at the bottom of the stairs; Naomi rested on her hip. Ruth returned. Mother said, 'Ungrateful child. Most children in Jamaica would give their eye teeth for what you've got.'

'Sorry, Mother.' She hung her head.

We went up to our tower in disgrace, watched the rain from the window, and awaited Father's return. Joshua stayed downstairs in the sitting-room, keeping Naomi company.

Father arrived home in a bad mood. The cricket was a washout. His footsteps quickened on the stairs. Ruth bit her nails. I twiddled the straightened fringe round my finger.

Father snarled, 'So you've disobeyed your mother and me?'

'What's so terrible about straightening our hair?'

99

Ruth hurled the words at Father. 'Mother does it all the time!'

Father unbuckled his belt. 'Right! You need to be taught a lesson. What your mother does is of no concern to you.'

We children had had the odd smack from our grandparents when we were really naughty, but certainly not a beating. Father went after Ruth who dropped her doll on the floor and ran round the room, screaming. The whole affair would have been comical if not for the menacing look on Father's face. He ran hither and thither, chasing Ruth who jumped on to the bed. The doll's house Grandpa had made for Ruth was on the floor. Father stepped on it and smashed it. He lashed out, hitting Ruth round the calves.

'Grandpa, Grandpa, save me . . .' Ruth sobbed.

I was so angry, I cried, 'You've broken up her doll's house. Grandpa made it for her. You've broken it. I hate you, Father. Why couldn't you have left us with Grandma?'

Father flew into a rage. He swung round and lashed out at me, hitting my arms. I hollered: 'Grandma, Grandma, save me.'

'Leave her alone,' Ruth snarled. 'We hate you, Father. Why did you have to send for us, why?'

'You're out of order.' Father lashed out, hitting the bed. He held the belt in mid air and said in patois: 'Look yah, pickney; dohn provoke me!'

'Sorry, Daddy.' Eye-water tumbled down Ruth's cheeks. Father had never spoken harshly to her, let alone belted her. 'Sorry, Daddy. I didn't mean to upset you.'

Father always gave in to Ruth whenever she called him 'Daddy'. He stood there staring at her calves; angry weals rose up. 'Sorry, Princess. I could cut off my right hand.'

'Oh, Father.' Ruth stared at his right hand.

Father had a way of making you feel guilty. He turned. 'And what have you got to say for yourself, Hope?' A frown clouded Father's face.

'We didn't mean to upset you, Father.' I lowered my eyes to where the broken doll's house sat on the floor. Ruth's doll lay on its back, eyes closed, hair sprawled. 'We're sorry, Father. We won't do it again.'

Father gave a belly sigh. 'You children would try the patience of a saint.'

Mother stood in the doorway. Her facial muscles twitched. She had left us to the mercy of the leather belt. I resented the beating. I wanted to run away from home.

'Go into the bathroom, girls. I'm going to wash your hair. Let's hope you haven't damaged the follicles.'

Father picked up the belt, composed himself. 'You girls should know better. Straightened hair is for grown women.'

'Yes, Father.'

After Mother had washed our hair, bathed Ruth's calves and my arms in salt water, we were ordered to sit quietly and watch the film, *To Sir With Love*. Father had read the book, written by a West Indian writer Edward Braithwaite; the film starred Sidney Poitier and Lulu. It was set in the East End: a black teacher trying to control a class of unruly children.

Mother dried my hair while Father attempted to put Ruth's doll's house back together.

'This is a bit like putting Humpty Dumpty together.' Father held a screwdriver. 'It took ages to put it together at Christmas, now I can't seem to fit the pieces together again.'

Joshua galloped his wooden horse, Gideon, on the surface of the mahogany coffee table. Meantime Naomi shook the side of her playpen, reaching out to Joshua.

'I hate to see her in that pen.' Joshua crawled over to Naomi. 'If you ask me, playpens are like pounds back home; you lock up animals in pounds when they trespass on your land.'

'Sh!' Father said. 'I'm trying to do two things at once: watch the TV and put this doll's house together.'

'That's enough of your opinion, young man.' Mother combed the knots out of my hair. 'Lord, your hair is tough, Hope. I think I'll run it through with my straightening comb.'

'But that's not fair,' Ruth said. 'What about me?'

Father shut her up by raising his right hand. 'I'm watching the film, Princess.'

'I was just saying,' Mother said, 'I'm going to straighten Hope's hair, make it more manageable.'

Father held the screwdriver. He turned to Mother. 'I don't believe you, Beatrice.' (Mother was called Beatrice whenever she fell from grace.) 'You caused me to chastise the girls and now you're going back on your word.'

'I'm not,' Mother said. 'Hope's hair is really tough; I'm just trying to make it more manageable.'

Alleluia! I had visions of sitting in front of the mirror brushing my long silky hair. Ruth cut her eyes on me.

Father stared at the credits on the television, saying: 'Yes, sir, Sidney Poitier is my man; he's made it.'

'By the way, Jasper,' Mother said, 'you haven't forgotten we're going out tonight?'

'I'm not sure I want to go,' Father said.

'We'll have to go, Jasper,' Mother said. 'Captain Sprat specifically invited us to his show.'

'Captain Sprat?' Joshua cooed at Naomi: 'Abu-bu-bu. Captain Sprat sounds a bit fishy to me.'

'You can say that again,' Father said. 'We met him at the Jamaican High Commission the other day. He's a limbo dancer. He's putting on a show at Clapham Manor Baths tonight.'

'It's not fair,' Joshua said. 'You and Mother are always going out. We went everywhere with Grandma and Grandpa.'

Father put the damaged doll's house aside, lifted Naomi from the playpen. 'Joshua, your mother and I are under a lot of pressure at work. We need to relax occasionally.'

'I suppose Mrs Parsons will be looking after us?'

'Who else?' Father said. 'Bunty is our right-hand. You couldn't ask for a better neighbour.'

Mother said, 'I wonder what the new neighbours on our left will be like? I'm so used to that house being empty. Let's hope they're nice and friendly like Bunty.'

'I don't care what they're like as long as they're

not riff-raff,' Father said. 'Let's talk about something else.'

'I'm thinking of applying for a new job, Jasper.' Mother changed the subject. 'I've seen an advert in the local paper for trainee nurses at St Stephen's Hospital.'

'You must be joking!' Father was almost hysterical.

'It's better than being the office tea lady,' Mother said.

Father said, 'Nursing is not in my league, Beatrice! Don't forget the kind of life we were used to back home.' Father's voice hit the roof. 'If I were in Jamaica now I'd have a chauffeur, a yard-boy and a nanny for the children.'

'It's all coming out now,' Mother said. 'Heaven help me.'

'All I want is the life we used to have back home. I don't like being treated as a second class citizen.'

The rain beat on the window panes and Father's bucket overflowed. Thunder roared and lightning flashed. Naomi screamed. Father shoved her in Mother's arms, kicked the broken doll's house out of the way, almost knocking me over in the assault.

'I'll finish plaiting your hair later, Hope,' Mother said. 'I'll see if I can mend the doll's house tomorrow, Ruth.'

Joshua muttered: 'When you hear thunder and lightning you know the devil and his wife are fighting over mackerel water.'

'Enough of your nonsense, boy!' Father barked. 'I don't know why people teach children such silly nonsense back home.'

'I wish I was back home,' Ruth said. 'I hate it here.'

'You children are spoilt,' Mother said. 'You have no consideration for anyone except your grandparents.'

'If I had my life again . . .' Father's words hung in limbo. He left the room wearing a hard expression.

'If I didn't have these children I'd be off, too.' Mother flung her words at the door. She cooed, sat Naomi on her lap, sighing: 'If I had my life again, I'd have only one child . . .'

The words pierced our flesh.

Father returned with a handful of white shirts, threw them on the sofa. 'What am I going to wear tonight, Beatrice?'

'Oh, don't bother me, Jasper,' Mother said. 'You know where the iron is kept.'

'What is the world coming to when a man has to iron his own shirt?' Father frowned. 'Hope, go and iron this shirt for me. I presume you know how to iron?'

'Yes, Father,' I said. 'Grandma taught me.'

Father said, 'Joshua, go and polish my shoes. And can you make sure I've got clean handkerchiefs, Ruth.'

We took our orders seriously. As we climbed the stairs, Father said, 'I'm sorry, Bea. I don't know what came over me.'

'I don't know what's happening to us,' Mother said. 'Everything has changed since the children came.'

'Too many mouths depending on me, Bea,' Father

said. 'It makes me irritable. I wish we didn't have so many children.'

'It's not my fault,' Mother said.

There was a feeling of being unwanted. Resentment festered and the scabby wound I'd been nursing opened. Oh, to have wings like a dove. I wanted to fly away. Instead I decided to run away. Then there'd be one less mouth to feed.

We were delivered to Mrs Parsons' house. Naomi was installed in the box room which she slept in during the day. Joshua would join her later. Ruth and I were to sleep in the room next to Mrs Parsons', on the second floor. There was an oval-shaped mirror in the hallway. It hung from a tarnished chain. Mother had forgotten to straighten my hair. The plaits were going east, west. I didn't care much for my reflection.

Mrs Parsons said, 'I'm going to make Welsh rabbit for supper. How does that sound?'

'Yum, yum; we're going to eat rabbits from Wales,' Joshua said. 'I've never eaten rabbit meat.'

'No, no!' Mrs Parsons' hands shot up to her cheeks. 'It's just another word for toasted cheese on buttered toast.'

We children admired ornaments on the mantlepiece in the sitting-room. Mrs Parsons went off to the kitchen, humming.

'I feel silly,' Joshua said. 'Welsh rabbit, I ask you.'

Ruth and I giggled. We gave ourselves stitches, laughing.

Finally Mrs Parsons returned, saying, 'Give us a hand, girls. Supper's ready.'

After we'd settled ourselves with four trays on our knees, mouths watering at the sight of Welsh rabbit, Mrs Parsons said, 'Why were you girls screaming earlier on.'

'Father was angry with us,' Ruth said. 'He belted us.'

'Oh, dear; I don't believe in smacking children.'

'Can you teach me how to play chopsticks, please, Mrs Parsons?' Ruth asked after we'd finished our supper. (There was a large piano over by the bay window.) 'All the girls at school can play chopsticks.'

Mrs Parsons said, 'Why not. Yes. I'll teach you how to play; that will keep me occupied in the evenings. But right now I feel like having a good old-fashioned singsong.'

We sang 'When the red, red robin comes bob, bob, bobbin' along', and 'I love to go a-wandering'.

The raindrops battered the window pane and the music failed to heal my wound. I tried to forgive Father, but I couldn't forget the beating. And the thought of being unwanted pierced my wound further. I studied Mrs Parson's transparent skin (the wrinkles round her mouth, the clear blue eyes) as she played the piano and sang "Val-de ha ha ha ha ha". In that moment it was easy to pretend we children were at home, sitting up in Grandma and Grandpa's bed singing a medley.

'Good night, dears.' Mrs Parson closed the lid of the piano. 'Brush your teeth before you go to bed . . .'

*

'Wot you doing out on a night like this?' A shadow came reeling towards me. It drank from a bottle, belched and said, 'You've knicked my spot. That's where I kip at night.'

When I first thought of running away, I had notions of packing my grip, finding a nice comfortable place to live. Clapham Common was as far as I got, for the rain had dissolved into a drizzle, dampening my courage. There I sat huddled into the safety of a tree trunk, regretting my act of defiance. I knew nothing about survival in the open, knew not where to go. Droplets of water hung from the overhead branches like diamonds. I rose, made a dash but the man caught my arm.

'Get off me. Leave me alone.' The predictable words fought their way, kicked, struggled.

'Doing a runner, are yer?' His breath reeked of alcohol. 'Well, you picked the wrong night, silly goose.'

'Let go of me, mister. I've done nothing wrong.'

'You must be running from the bogey man then.'

'You're the bogey man!'

'Cheeky little madam.' He released my arm, bedded down in his space. 'There's enough room for two.' He hiccupped.

'No thank you.' I ran off, hid in a telephone kiosk.

'Oi, get out of my space.' A shadow kicked the kiosk.

I whimpered, scrambled to my feet when I saw an old woman, carrying the world in two carrier bags, glaring at me.

'Don't just stand there! Get lost, kid. Buzz off!'

I found myself wandering in the middle of the night. I knew not where to turn, that was until I passed a petrol station where a shadow got into a car, drove towards me and stopped: 'Lost, are you, love? Want a lift?' He tempted me, saying: 'Come on, love; have a wine gum.'

I thought of Sweetie Man, and then I took flight into the night, only this time there was no wall to jump over. I ran straight into the headlights of a squad car.

I was questioned, delivered home in the early hours of the morning. The police cautioned Father about child abuse.

'I've been in this country for five years and I've never been in trouble with the law until today. If you ever do such a thing again I'll turn you over to the social services, let them look after you,' Father said after the police had left.

'I don't know what came over the child,' Mother said.

'What would Mama and Papa say if you went and got yourself killed? It would send them to an early grave.'

'Sorry, Mother, Father; it won't happen again.'

'Just wait till your grandparents hear about this,' Mother said. 'They'll write and give you a ticking off.'

'This is our problem, Bea,' Father said.

'She needs a good hiding,' Mother said.

'The law in this country is on the side of the children,' Father said. 'Parental control has been taken away.'

'Well, the next time she runs away,' Mother said,

'the police can jolly well take her to the social services. See how she likes living in a children's home.'

There was no 'welcome back'; 'thank God you're safe' from my parents. My flight into the night had brought wrath upon my head. Off I went up the stairs in the dark.

'Mrs Parsons called the police when she found you gone,' Ruth said. 'She came and checked on us in the middle of the night. We were all sick with worries.'

'Thank God you're safe.' Joshua bounced on the bed. 'You had Mrs Parsons really worried. She had to take a tablet to relax her when Mother and Father came home. She kept blaming herself, said you'd probably fallen into the wrong hands.'

'You'll have to go over and apologise first thing in the morning,' Ruth said. 'Fancy running away. That was my plan. You beat me to it. Were you scared?' She giggled.

'Yes,' I said. 'Don't even think about it.'

We children huddled on the bed, heads together as though in conspiracy. It was good to be home. We were lucky to have a solid foundation, but it didn't seem that way at the time. Ruth and Joshua were soon asleep. I drifted off to sleep with Grandma's words in my ear: 'When in Rome you do as the Romans to, Hope; adopt the ways of the people, settle down.' I slept on her words, cradled them in my bosom, for I knew I had to settle down, grasp opportunity.

Saints and Sinners

Dear Grandma,

Greetings to you and Grandpa and all the animals on the farm. Say howdy-do to everyone for me, especially Aunt Enid, Aunt Esme and Uncle Ely. Ruth and Joshua send love, too.

Oh Grandma, I must tell you about my cho-cho vine. I had it in a pot on the window sill in the kitchen. It has grown so much, I've transferred it to a shady corner in the garden. Now the vine is growing up a barren apple tree. I don't suppose it will bear cho-chos, but I don't mind. It comes from the soil in Jamaica. That is enough for me.

I must tell you what happened to me at school the other day. I sat in the classroom listening to Sister Julie, our form teacher, talking about the end of term project. You had to choose a famous person: Florence Nightingale, Joan of Arc, Mother Teresa, Golda Meir, Ghandi, King Henry VIII, Hitler . . .

There's a Japanese girl in my class called Yoko. She chose Gladys Aylward, the missionary who took all those Chinese children across the Yellow River in China during the Second World War.

I was really surprised when I heard Gladys Aylward's name. Remember how we children listened in awe as Grandpa read aloud about

Gladys Aylward's adventures in China: the time when there was a prison riot and one of the prisoners went mad, hacking at the inmates with an axe, shouting 'Aieee! Aieee...' Only Gladys could calm him down. She did many good deeds for the villagers, too.

Sister Julie said, 'Well, Hope, Yoko has already chosen Gladys Aylward. Why don't you do something on slavery?'

I became self-conscious when a girl called Maeve said, 'Sister, are all West Indians descended from slaves?'

Sister Julie found the answer somewhat tricky. She said: 'Well, yes, I suppose so. They are the descendants of the slaves who were brought over from Africa to work...'

You can imagine how I felt, Grandma. All eyes settled on me. Then Sister Julie said: 'Come to think of it, Hope, you should be able to get a lot of information from Lavender Hill Library: for a start most of the influential abolitionists, William Wilberforce, John Wesley, etc, lived in Clapham. They were nicknamed the saints, and known as the Clapham Sect. Why, we have history on our doorstep.'

I refused to do my project on slavery. It's all very well being descended 'from a proud African tribe', as Grandpa used to say, but in England nearly everyone looks down on Africans. I said to Sister Julie, 'But I'd prefer to write about Gladys Aylward. I used to read about her when I was in Jamaica.'

Sister Julie shrugged her shoulders: 'Very well,

it's your project; do what you like.' I've decided to
write a kind of poem-project: I'm going to draw
pictures of you and Grandpa, the animals on the
farm at home and a picture of the Blue Mountains
in Jamaica, too. The poem goes like this:

> Grandma said 'When in Rome you do as the
>   Romans do.'
> I Carried a picture of baby Jesus in a manger.
> And Grandpa said 'Don't forget to visit London
>   Zoo.'
> Then I realised I was about to become a stranger.
>
> When finally we arrived in foreign land,
> Ruth made a wish at one of the fountains
> In Trafalgar Square where Joshua tugged at my
>   hand
> As I stood remembering the Blue Mountains.
>
> Low and behold we'd arrived in the big city,
> Shivering and yearning to go home,
> Thinking, Lord, Lord, what a pity;
> But alas we were in Rome.

Do you like it, Grandma?
I forgot to mention one serious problem,
Grandma: last month I noticed pink stains on my
panties. I hid them from Mother. What does it
mean?
I close with love, Grandma. Write soon.
                    Your same,
                    Hope.

Our household was a volatile place, for Father's

blood had a habit of boiling. Woe betide anyone who crossed him. I was still wearing sackcloth and ashes because I'd caused the law to caution Father. He reminded me over and over again that he had never brought shame on my grandparents. In fact, as a child, he was a goody-goody, known as an all-rounder at school: he was top of his class and captain of the cricket team.

'Hope.' Father wagged my school report in my face. 'What the devil is this? You've come bottom of the class.'

'Don't burst a blood vessel, Jasper,' Mother said. 'It's her first school report; we've got to give her time.'

We were sitting round the dining-table in the kitchen. We'd just eaten a meal of red peas soup with yams, sweet potatoes, dumplings and salt beef.

'Give her time, my foot!' Father said. 'The child has had nine months to settle in. Why, when I was her age I'd passed all my exams; I was on my way to high school . . .'

Mother was still feeding Naomi mashed pumpkin in red peas soup. She said. 'We can't all be as bright as you, Jasper: head cook and chief bottle-washer.'

Father snarled, 'Look here, Beatrice! Our children are loggerheads, and all you can do is humour me. First I read Joshua's report: he spends half his time playing. Ruth's labelled a chatter-box. Hope is a dunce. In my day it was a disgrace to come anything but first, second or third in class. Lord, I can't stand loggerhead-birds. They fly aimlessly all over the place: hither and thither, no sense of direction.'

Naomi blew raspberries, soup dribbling down her chin.

Father said, 'When I was six years old I made my parents proud. I recited a verse from the Second Book of Samuel:

'The beauty of Israel is slain
Upon thy high places:
How are the mighty fallen . . .

Saul and Jonathan were lovely
And pleasant in their lives,
And in their death they were not divided:
they were swifter than eagles,
They were stronger than lions . . .'

'I learnt so many Bible verses when I was a child, they're coming out of my ears.' Mother finished feeding Naomi and put the dishes in the sink. She turned to me. 'Seriously, Hope, we're very upset about you running away. You embarrassed your father and me in front of the police.'

'Sorry, Mother, Father.'

'Apology accepted.' Father's voice was deep. 'Mark you, just this once. If it happens again I'll tan your hide.'

'Enough said, Jasper,' Mother interrupted. 'And another thing, Hope, your teachers say you spend half your time daydreaming. What's this I hear about you refusing to do a project on slavery? Your form teacher said she asked you to do that project because you were "born in Jamaica which has a history of slavery". She thought you'd rise to the challenge.'

'I'm not sure I agree with this Sister Julie, Beatrice,' Father said. 'Slavery was soul-destroying; I don't want my children getting an inferiority complex because of slavery.'

Mother poured washing up liquid in the sink. 'It sounds as if you want to sever all ties with Africa, Jasper.'

'You know that's not true, Beatrice,' Father said. 'I do admire Africans: even when their left foot is resting on the graveyard wall, they've got a book in their right hand.'

'Kiff, kiff, kiff,' Ruth and Joshua giggled.

'I'm going to wipe that smile off your faces in a minute.' Father stared at Ruth and Joshua.

Everyone jumped when the door knocked: Joshua's friends wanted to know if he could play out.

'Send those children away from my door, Joshua!' Father said. 'Go to your room and take up your book. I will not have you running round the streets like an unthinking horse . . .'

Joshua's friends went away. He climbed the stairs, vexed.

'Can I go to the pictures with my friends on Saturday, Daddy?' Ruth asked. 'Please, Daddy.'

'No, you can't,' Father said. 'Go to your room and take up a book. "Give to life the best you can and the best will come back to you . . ." '

'Your father is right,' Mother said. ' "Good, better, best; never let it rest, until your good be

116

better, and your better be best". That's what our teachers used to say at home.'

'Oh!' Ruth dragged out the word, left the table. 'I'm tired of those old sayings.'

'I'll give you old saying in a minute, miss lady,' Father snapped. 'You children think life is a merry-go-round.'

'That's not fair, Father,' I said. 'I do lots of chores round the house and I'm never allowed to go out.'

'After all the botheration you've caused,' Father said, 'I'm surprised you've got the gall to complain.'

'Sorry, Father.' I carried the crockery to the sink with trembling hands. I dropped a plate.

'Be-eee careful, Hope,' Mother dragged the words. 'First you ruin my forks; now you've broken one of my good plates.'

'Sorry, Mother,' I said. 'I wasn't paying attention.'

Father picked up the pieces. 'That's the trouble with you: you're always daydreaming or writing secret letters to your grandparents. I trust you haven't written and told them about your little escapade?'

'No, Father.'

There was a sigh of relief. 'Good. I don't want you upsetting Mama and Papa. Do you hear me?'

'Yes, Father.'

'We got a letter from home today,' Mother said. 'Your grandparents are concerned about you, Hope. They say you're not getting on with the girls at school; is that right?'

'What's all this nonsense about you being bullied?' Father said. 'If you are having problems

117

at school you are supposed to let us know, not your grandparents.'

'It's these girls at school, they keep picking on me . . .'

'Right,' Father said. 'Names; I want their names! I'm going to write to the headmistress. I will not have my children being bullied. No sir. I won't stand for it.'

I was tempted to tell Father to sit down. Instead I said, 'Everything is all right now. I clipped one of the bullies' wings. They won't bother me again.'

'Dat's my gal.' Father spoke a diluted form of patois. 'When me was your age me could throw a punch, yuh see . . .'

'I'm surprised at you, Jasper.' Mother laughed. 'I thought you were a model pupil.'

'The playground is a wilderness, Bea,' Father said. 'The devil is always flying around. If you don't defend yourself, He'll beat you with his wings, destroy your soul . . .'

'For someone who refuses to carry the Bible on his head, Jasper,' Mother said, 'you're certainly Biblical today.'

Father was a strange man: one minute he refused to speak in patois, next minute he was throwing patois and punches in the air, making jokes, saying, 'Show 'em who's boss, Cassius Clay: buff, buff, buff; a lef' hook 'ere, a right hook dere.'

'I'd put my money on Sonny Liston anytime,' Mother said.

'Seriously, Hope,' Father said, 'whenever anyone tries to make you feel inferior, remember this: our foreparents may have been slaves, but they resisted slavery to the bitter end; became landowners after abolition. Great-Aunt Minnie's brother Manroot had the manner and bearing of a king, a real storyteller. Your grandma has the voice of an angel. Your Grandpa's people were craftsmen; he himself is a sculptor. I take my hat off to our people.'

'I thought you wanted to forget slavery?'

'I just don't want to romanticize it, Bea,' Father said.

'Incidentally, Hope,' Mother said, 'your form teacher says you want to be a writer when you grow up. Is that so?'

'Yes,' I said coyly.

'But I've never ever seen you take up pen and ink,' Father said. 'Most writers have been writing since childhood.'

'Not necessarily, Jasper,' Mother said. 'Some people take up writing late in life. Anyway, she writes her grandparents all the time. I suppose you could say she's made a start.'

'It's good to hang your basket high,' Father said. 'But there's no money in writing, not for our people; you'll be sucking salt all your life. What you need is a solid foundation. Then you can choose: lawyer, doctor, dentist . . .'

'Don't put the child off.' Mother threw a tea-towel in my direction. 'In this life you have to fight for what you want.'

'Fight is not the word.' Father tossed the tea-towel in my direction. He lifted Naomi from the chair, took her into the sitting-room, saying: 'Oh, well, time will tell. They do say the pen is mightier than the sword.'

'Your father is bursting with old sayings.' Mother laughed. Then she added, 'I'm going to straighten your hair after we've put the cutlery and crockery away, Hope.'

'Alleluia!'

There was never a dull moment in our house. Ruth and Joshua had been banished upstairs, sulking. Father and Naomi were in the sitting-room, undoubtedly crawling round the room. (As high and mighty as Father was, he often crawled round the room, grunting, chasing Naomi.) I helped Mother to dry the dishes, daydreaming: I recalled Great-Aunt Minnie saying to Joshua: 'Labour for learning before you grow old, for learning is better than silver and gold . . .' The words swam round in my head. I had to do better at school, get a good education if I wanted to do my people justice.

11

The Visitor

It was assembly time. Sister Bernadette said she had
to go home to Ireland urgently: her ageing mother
was poorly and asking for her; she wanted to be at
her bedside at the end.

'Those of you who are going abroad for your
holiday, keep out of the sun, wear wide-brimmed
hats to protect delicate skin on the beach. For those
staying at home: play safe and go to mass as usual.
And for the sixth formers who are off to Lourdes,
safe journey and do bring back some holy water
for friends and relatives who are sick in body, mind
and spirit.'

'Thank you, Sister Bernadette,' everyone
chorused.

The hall was hot and humid, for July had blazed
in with a vengeance. Girls shifted on their feet,
desperate to escape into the airy playground.

The assembly ended with a song. Sister Philippa
played the guitar. Sister Bernadette nodded in tune.
We sang 'Awake my soul and with the sun.'

'Leave the hall quietly, girls,' Sister Bernadette
said. 'No giggling, gossiping or loitering in the
corridors.'

We made our way to the classrooms, obeying
Sister Bernadette.

'Good morning, girls,' Sister Julie said.

'Good morning, Sister Julie.'

She took roll call, put the register away. Then she said: 'I see we have a birthday girl in our midst; let us wish Hope a happy twelfth birthday.'

'Happy Birthday, Hope!'

'I suppose you're all dying to find out the winner of the end of year project?' Sister Julie said. 'Louise Pink is the winner. She produced a first class piece of work on the life and times of St Vincent de Paul, 1575–1660. He was captured by African pirates shortly after being ordained a priest and was sold into slavery . . .'

My heart sank when Sister Julie's eyes sought me out. She said, 'Hope, I don't recall asking you to write a poem. When in school you do as the teacher says; don't you agree?'

'Yes, Sister.' I hung my head in shame. 'Sorry.'

Sister Julie's eyes moved on, settled on Louise, a skinny dark-haired girl who suffered with catarrh; she sat blowing her nose and smiling.

'Well done, Louise,' Sister Julie said. 'There's no runner-up prize, but I must commend one or two names: Maeve, your project on Mother Teresa of Calcutta was well-researched. Jasmine, your project on Ghandi was very good. Sylvia, I made a note of your comments: "St Francis of Assisi was a friend of animals and birds alike; he called them his brothers and sisters." Well written,' Sister Julie added.

There were sighs and long faces in the classroom.

'I must say, girls, all the projects were commendable . . .' Sister Julie attempted to soothe wounded egos.

At break, the bullies gathered in the playground. Maeve and her posse joined forces with Lisa and her gang. They were accomplices now. They were no longer names to me, just the posse. They prowled the schoolyard looking for weak-willed individuals. They found a scapegoat in Jasmine, a Kenyan girl. The posse bullied her into skipping with them. She got tangled up in the skipping rope, tripped, fell, got up and brushed off her grazed knees, wincing.

'Silly moo,' the posse said. 'You'll have to do better next time.' They approached Avril and me, smiling.

Jasmine stood there gazing like a gazelle. She was medium height and skinny with a thick head of hair. She wore glasses and her skin was nearly a dark as mine. But like Yoko, she ignored me, desperate to fit in.

'Oi, Byfield,' the posse said, 'we're going to give you the bumps.'

I cut my eyes on the spiteful faces which leered at me: 'One, two, three, four, five, six, seven.' The sky came down to greet me as the girls threw me up in the air.

'Put me down, put me down.' I struggled.

Any commotion in the playground drew a crowd. They were relieved not to be the victim of the posse. They shouted: 'Eight, nine, ten, eleven, twelve. Hip, hip, hooray.'

I was set down on wobbly feet. My stomach somersaulted and I fought nausea. I was gripped with stomach cramps.

'You look kind of greyish. What's the matter, scared?'

My hair was ruffled. Mother had straightened it, warned me to wear it tied back. I wanted long shiny hair; I had taken the ponytail clip out as soon as I was out of sight of home. Now it was all messed up.

'Let's go and pick on Yoko.' The posse moved on.

'What did you do to your hair?' Avril asked.

Skinny Louise had been standing with her back against the wall, reading *Little Women* by Louisa M. Alcott. She joined us. Lately she'd been hanging around Avril, telling her about the saga of Meg, Jo, Beth and Amy, the characters in the book she was reading. Avril, who hated reading, took it all in. She and I weren't exactly bosom pals, but she was all I had; I didn't fancy walking up and down the schoolyard at break alone.

'Yes. What did you do to your hair?' Louise asked.

'I had it straightened.'

'It looks funny, sticking up all over the place like a hedgehog's hair.' Avril's laughter stretched our friendship.

'It does, doesn't it?' Louise surveyed me from head to toe. I disliked her instantly.

'Oi, Byfield.' The posse returned. 'Lend us a tanner, will you? We want to go to the tuckshop.'

'I haven't got any money,' I said.

'Empty your pockets,' they said. 'Or else . . .'

'Leave me alone,' I snapped.

'Let's give her the bumps again!' I was hoisted

off my feet, thrown in the air so many times that I saw myself flying up to meet the clouds. I screamed, made myself hoarse. The crowd came to look at the birthday girl. I closed my eyes, stiffened my body, gave myself over to the posse.

'What's going on?' Sister Helen, the carbolic-smelling nun, was on playground duty. 'Put her down at once!'

I stood on weakened calves. Avril and Louise were red-faced. They were afraid of the posse.

'What's going on?' Sister Helen's eyes shot out at the posse. 'I'm waiting.'

'Nothing, Sister,' they said. 'We were giving Hope the bumps. It's her birthday today.'

'She didn't sound as if she was enjoying it,' Sister Helen said. 'You girls go too far sometimes.' She blew the whistle. 'Go and line up, single file.'

At lunch-time I was afraid to leave my seat. Twice I'd asked to be excused from the classroom but the temporary English teacher, Miss Worth, (Sister Julie, a diabetic, was in hospital,) wore a stony face, saying: 'Nobody spends a penny in my time.'

'But I don't want to spend a penny, Miss,' I'd said. 'I want to go to the toilet.'

'Silly girl! Where are you from? Spending a penny means you want to go to the loo; it's an English saying!'

Everyone giggled. Finally Miss Worth dismissed the class.

'Coming, Louise?' Avril crossed the room, stopped at Louise's desk. 'You will be coming next week, won't you? Only it's my birthday and I'm having a party.'

First I knew of Avril's birthday party. Like everything in my life, the slap on the face came suddenly.

'Don't just sit there, what's-your-name,' Miss Worth said after the others had rushed off to queue up in the dinner hall.

'I've got a stomach ache, miss.'

'Go and see the nurse,' she said impatiently.

I rose, walked towards the door.

'I see you've started your period,' Miss Worth said. 'Go to the sick room.' Her cold brown eyes, thin features brought a chill to my bones in the sweltering July afternoon.

'What's the matter, Byfield?' I met Sister Martha long the corridor. 'Why are you walking so stiffly.?'

'I've soiled my dress, Sister.'

'Oh, you poor child. Your visitor has arrived.' She inspected my summer dress. 'Come with me.'

We crossed the hall. Sister Martha put an arm round my shoulders. It was the most embarrassing moment of my life. Those who sat nearest the door drew their breaths, held it.

'You'll have to eat in the sick room,' Sister Martha said. 'I'll get Sister Brigid, the school nurse, to explain what is happening. She'll give you a letter to take home to your mother and a pad or two to tie you over until you get home.' She blew upwards, cooling her damp brow. 'She'll also rinse your dress out; in this heat it will dry before lunch is over.'

'Thank you, Sister,' I said.

'Think nothing of it. I've done this job a hundred times.' Sister Martha knocked on a white door.

I was delivered into the hands of a red-faced nun. Sister Martha explained the problem in a lowered voice.

Sister Brigid said: 'Don't worry; I'll soon have her cleaned up; Dr White's will put her right.'

'Thank you, Sister.' My cheeks burned with embarrassment.

The next lesson was music.

'As it's coming up to the end of term,' Sister Philippa said, 'I thought we'd have a sing-song.'

'Oh,' the posse groaned. 'Can't we do something else?'

'Just one song to exercise the vocal chords.' Sister Philippa strummed the guitar. 'Then we can talk.' She sang 'Saul went out to sow his seeds'.

The posse interrupted. 'Oh, can't we do something else? Singing is boring. Let's talk about the birds and the bees?'

'That's not my subject,' Sister Philippa said.

'How do babies come?' the girls asked.

'Well,' Sister Philippa strummed the guitar. 'The stork brings them, leaves them under the gooseberry bush.'

'Ah, ah, ah!' the girls who knew better chorused.

Sister Philippa twanged the guitar string: 'We are all friends here, friends share secrets; isn't that so, girls?'

'Yes, Sister!'

'Well, I'm going to let you in on a well-kept secret,' Sister Philippa said in a hushed voice. 'When a girl reaches puberty she bleeds; we call it menstruation or her period. When she gets married, she and her husband celebrate the sacrament of marriage by coupling – having sex. When the sperm from the man and the egg from the woman meet, they fuse – fertilise. That's how babies are made. After nine months in the mother's womb, nature expels the baby from the expectant mother's body through the birth canal: the vagina.'

'Ugh!' Hands flew up, covered mouths.

So that was how Dominic's chicks came about. But then she didn't give birth. The eggs were hatched. And the mares in Grandpa's corral . . . It all came back to me now. Grandpa had said one of his mares was with foal. Ruth had asked him if the mare had mated with a fowl. How foolish we were then. Grandpa bred horses as a living. Why hadn't Grandma told me the facts of life? Why did she let me find out like this?

Sister Philippa said, 'I hope I didn't shock anyone? You're all young ladies now; it's time you knew the truth.'

There was silence, the odd cough, saliva being swallowed. The grand piano, the drums, the xylophones, the tambourines, the flutes bore witness, played silent music on our behalf.

Sister Philippa strummed the guitar again. We sang 'No man is an island'.

Our next lesson was PE. Sister Philippa became the favourite teacher of the day; she had opened our eyes.

'Anyone who's having a period is excused from games,' Sister Philippa said. 'It's a hot day and I don't want anyone fainting in the playground. We're playing rounders today.'

I sat on a bench in the schoolyard thinking, just

128

my luck; I'm always on display. Why me? Meantime blonde haired Mary, who was due to emigrate to Australia, and Venetia who spoke in a 'la-di-da fashion', as the posse often said, sat on the bench rooting for their respective team.

'Go on, Maeve; hit the ball!' Mary was engrossed in the game. 'Go on; run, run . . .'

'This is my second period.' Venetia turned to me.

'I started today,' I said. 'I've got a terrible stomach ache. I feel so miserable.'

'Me too.' Venetia took her eyes off the game. 'That explains why Sister Martha was escorting you across the dinner hall in a hurry. Amy and I wondered what was going on.'

The time passed quickly. It wasn't long before Sister Philippa blew the whistle. We all lined up.

'You girls look like wilted flowers,' Sister Philippa said. 'A nice cool shower will revive you.'

Amy stripped off in the changing room, showered; then she sat on the bench next to Venetia and me. 'What kind of sanitary protection will you be using: tampons or towels?'

I was ignorant of sanitary protection, except for the one I was wearing. I stuttered, 'Towels, I suppose.'

Avril sat on the bench opposite with Louise, towels wrapped around them, talking. Our friendship ended where it began when Avril said, 'Don't wait for me, Hope. Louise's mother is giving me a lift. I'm having tea at their house.'

'OK.' It wasn't as if we were good friends: we didn't share secrets; I'd never been to her house.

As I walked out of the school gate, Amy and

Venetia strolled by. They gave a friendly wave: 'Have a nice weekend. Hope you feel better by Monday.' They climbed into their mothers' expensive-looking cars.

'Thanks.' I waved and smiled. The smile soon disappeared when Avril and Louise passed by, skinning their teeth at me. They climbed into a Jaguar. The driver was a skinny woman wearing dark glasses, white sundress, cork-soled sandals with straps going up her calves: Louise's mother. Avril and Louise giggled like bosom pals. The car drove off.

Sister Martha was on guard duty at the school gate. She nodded to a smiling policeman who came out of the station near by, crossed the road and headed towards Battersea Dogs' Home. She smiled. 'Good evening, Byfield. Chin up. Things will look different once you've made a few friends.'

'Good evening, Sister.'

Life was full of blows. I felt like the man in the Bible story who had been robbed and beaten. Two people passed him by without taking any action; a third took pity on him, cleaned his wound, gave him money. I set off on my journey home. I walked behind a group of girls who were laughing in a carefree manner; friendship was taken for granted: I thirsted after it, feeling as though I were walking in the wilderness alone.

12

Books are Friends

My favourite place in the school was the library. The posse rarely frequented this quiet area. But that was not the reason I liked the library. It was the view from the window. There was an allotment at the rear of the modern building. The caretaker, Mr Acres, lived in a cottage near by. He cultivated the land. I imagined the lanky man who tilled the soil, tended his vegetables, was Uncle Isaiah. There were wild flowers in the farthest corner of the allotment, too. Tranquility caught me in its hold, held me fast at the window where I watched the whole process of sowing and reaping.

'A penny for your thoughts.' Sister Mary-Ann tapped me on the shoulder on the last day of term. There was a free period because Sister Agnes, the RE teacher, was going to a religious retreat in Canterbury for the holidays. She wanted an early getaway. Sister Mary-Ann was a popular nun with a mischievous streak. She taught the older girls English, Typing and Office Practice. She mocked me in playful manner, reciting a verse Mr Trelawny, my old headmaster, often recited:

'What is this life, it's full of care.
I have no time to stand and stare ...'

131

'Sorry, Sister.' I turned, to be greeted by the scent of lily of the valley.

'Don't apologise. I shouldn't have crept up on you . . .'

Sister Mary-Ann almost caused a riot when she appeared in assembly minus her veil one morning. Girls craned their necks, nudging, whispering; they found it difficult to hold a song. At the time, Sister Mary-Ann was taking the sixth formers to Wimbledon to watch tennis. She wore a pastel-blue, turtle-neck sweater, navy calf-length skirt and a gold crucifix. She had cropped tobacco-coloured hair, fringed. When she sat on the platform and crossed her legs the hem of her white petticoat peeped out. The other nuns held themselves upright as though corseted. It was rumoured that Sister Mary-Ann had once been engaged. Her fiancé jilted her a few days before the wedding. She was idolised by the older girls: she had a romantic past; a real story-book heroine.

'What is it about that allotment that fascinates you so?' she whispered. 'It can't be Acres' slug-eaten cabbages.'

'I like to watch things grow, Sister.'

'Oh, yes, of course,' she said. 'I forgot you were born in rural Jamaica. Total contrast, wouldn't you say?'

'Yes, Sister.' I smiled. 'There are no fields, plants, animals, and the sky is always murky.'

'Ah! But we do get the odd rainbow and occasionally the sun puts its hat on and the blue sky smiles at us.'

My cheeks dimpled up. I stifled a grin.

'And what do you think of our library? Is there a library in your old school?'

'No, Sister. But the headmaster had a collection of books. The teachers read them to us.' I looked around the library. 'I can't imagine any school owning so many books.'

'And are you a member of the local library?'

'Yes, Sister. I've started going on Saturday afternoons. They've got all the fairy-stories I used to hear back home.'

'It must be wonderful to see them in book-form.'

'A miracle,' I said.

Every so often the older girls wandered in and out of the library. They wore their hair loose and some had open-neck shirts with their ties worn loosely. Of course, this was because Sister Bernadette was away. For all Sister Martha's strictness, she wasn't as eagle-eyed as Sister Bernadette.

'Let's take the weight off our feet.' Sister Mary-Ann gestured to a quiet corner. 'Whoops, I'm in trouble again; I can see Penelope frowning at me.'

Penelope was the tallest girl in the sixth-form. Her blonde hair was parted down the centre. Her tie was neatly done up, and a prefect badge was fastened to her cream cotton shirt. (First time I spoke to her I pronounced her name as 'Pene-lope', and felt so foolish when she corrected me.)

We sat at a table near the window.

'Sister Julie and Sister Agnes say you're very bright, Byfield, but it doesn't reflect in your work. What a pity.'

'I used to like school at home,' the words rushed out. 'But it's different here. I can't concentrate . . .'

'It's not easy finding yourself in a new country, a new school with lots of new faces. I remember how nervous I was when I became a novice at twenty-five years old. I kept wondering whether I'd fit in. I used to be a secretary before I took the vow.' She surveyed me. 'I see you haven't chosen a book as yet. *Heidi* is a wonderful book; so is Doris Lessing's *Nine African Stories*, set in South Africa.'

'I haven't chosen a book as yet, Sister, because I'm waiting for *This Time Next Week* by Leslie Thomas to be returned. Penelope said it's due back this afternoon.'

'Why not read all three over the holidays? Better still, read as many books as possible, catch up with your classmates. Ask your local librarian for a list of classic books.'

'Yes. I will. Thank you, Sister.'

Sister Mary-Ann rose. 'Mustn't idle: lots of letters to type and send out. Sister Agnes and I are organising a skiing trip to Austria next Easter. I hope you'll be able to go.' She smiled. 'By the way, did you give your mother that letter from Sister Brigid? I suggest you carry an extra pad in your satchel from now on. It happens to the best of us, especially the first time; don't be embarrassed.'

So she knew my visitor had arrived, knew all there was to know about me. I forgot she helped out in the office whenever the school secretary was sick or on holiday.

'Have a good holiday.' Sister Mary-Ann skipped

off, reminding me of a carefree goat-kid, dancing round its mother.

'We've been looking for you.' Venetia and Amy's faces had taken on a rosy glow. The hated word 'tan' was in fashion. The posse kept comparing their brown arms, giggling; they made me conscious of my dark skin.

'Have you?' I replied. 'Why?' (Since the arrival of my visitor, the girls and I acknowledged each other in passing.)

'Would you like to come to my birthday party next Wednesday?' Venetia handed me a pink envelope.

I hesitated.

'Well?' Amy took in my trembling hands.

I asked myself why Venetia wanted me at her party? I wrestled with suspicion, tossed it aside. I wanted to shout: 'Yes, thank you!' Instead I said, 'I don't know. It depends on what my parents say.'

'My telephone number is on the invitation letter,' Venetia said. 'Once they've given the OK give me a ring.'

The words rushed out, spluttered all over the place; I fidgeted. 'W-we haven't got a telephone.'

'You haven't got a telephone!' Amy exclaimed.

'There must be call-box near you.' Venetia rose. 'See you later. I've got to find Antonia, Jane, Yoko and Sylvia; a few more invitations to give out.'

'Ask them nicely,' Amy added. 'If they say no, offer to do extra chores: cleaning the budgie's cage, taking the dog for a walk, making the beds or doing the washing up. It never fails. I can twist my parents round my little finger anytime.'

I fiddled with the envelope. 'Thanks for the advice.'

The girls went off on their errand. I left the library with *Heidi* and *Little House on the Prairie*. I wanted nothing to do with Africa; *Nine African Stories* stayed on the shelf. Leslie Thomas's *This Time Next Week* never arrived.

The children's section of the local library was reached from an alleyway off the main road. The houses in the surrounding area backed on to the alleyway. There were dustbins, motor-mechanic garages, mangy cats and hungry-looking dogs, too. The odd motorbike came revving down the footpath. You threw yourself onto the iron railings, which protected the basement windows in the library, to avoid being run over.

The interior of the library compensated for the perils that lay outside. There were round tables which seated six at a time. There was an open fire with a fire-guard. There were low shelves stacked with books. On the wall there was a poster saying ' "Peter and the Wolf", reading on tape.' The stone floor was tiled; you walked lightly to avoid disturbing the children who sat reading. It was here that we discovered the fairy-stories we'd grown up on (new stories, too). Old friends waited on the shelves to be re-acquainted with.

'Excuse me, miss,' Ruth said. 'Have you a copy of *A Treasury of Jamaican Poetry*?'

The librarian crossed the room. She wore a short-sleeved white blouse and a plaid, pleated skirt. She had sharp dark eyes and short curly hair. Her desk reminded me of a shop-counter; if she sat down you could only see the top of her head over the counter. On the desk there were stamp-pads, a bottle of ink, a pot of glue containing a brush. I took these things in on every visit, for I'd never seen such a place back home.

'I'm sorry, I can't say I've heard of that one. Was it published in this country?'

'But you must have,' Ruth protested. 'It's got loads of poems by Jamaican poets. I think it was published over here, for most of our books at home used to say "Longman Caribbean".'

'Oh, dear. I don't think I can help you,' the librarian said. 'Why don't you choose an English nursery rhyme book?'

'Excuse me, miss. Do you have a list of classic books?'

'A list of classic books!' The librarian's voice rose up to the ceiling in surprise.

'Yes, miss. I was told to ask you for a list . . .'

'Oh, I see. I'll give it to you later.' The librarian came down to earth and made her way back to her desk.

Joshua was busy leafing through a picture-book. It said, *Hiawatha* by H. W. Longfellow. He put it back on the shelf, ran his hand along the books. *A Child's Garden of Verses* by R. L. Stevenson. He leafed through the book, reciting: 'I have a little shadow that goes in and out with me . . .'

'Silence in the library, please,' the librarian said.

'Sorry, miss,' Joshua said.

'Yes, well; please observe the rules,' the librarian said.

I gave Joshua a stern look, put a finger to my lip.

'I can't help it if the words jump out of my mouth,' Joshua said. 'I never expected to see "My Shadow" by R. L. Stevenson again. I just couldn't help reciting it.'

'Shush,' Ruth said. 'The librarian is watching us.'

We chose our books and seated ourselves in silence.

Father sat on the sofa in the sitting-room leafing through his latest book. He'd just finished reading *Minty Alley* by C. L. R. James, set in Trinidad in the early part of the century. Now he was reading *Banjo* by the Jamaican writer Claude McKay, about West Indian and African immigrants living in France during the 1930s. Unlike Mother, who only ever read the *Reader's Digest*, Father loved reading books by West Indian writers; he kept quoting: 'Books are friends, come let us read.'

There were two letters on the coffee table. A new cut-glass vase displayed fresh flowers. I sat on the floor cleaning the silver Cousin Archie and Aunt Jemima had given me, for it had turned black. Father put the book aside and read the invitation from Venetia. Mother was darning a pair of Joshua's trousers. Ruth and Joshua played scrabble on the floor. Naomi was sleeping upstairs in her cot.

'An invitation, eh?' Father waved the pink envelope at me.

'Please, Father, can I go?' I said. 'I've never been invited to a party before. Please say yes.'

'Whoa!' Father said. 'No one said anything about

you not going. It's just that I don't know these people from Adam: what does her father do for a living, and her mother, too?'

'I once overheard Venetia saying her father was an insurance broker in the City. Her mother doesn't work. She collects her from school in a big car. I promised to ring her from a call-box to tell her your decision.'

Father checked the address, smiled. 'Chelsea. Why, we're practically neighbours. You'll return the RSVP by post.'

'Why can't we have a phone?' Ruth asked. 'All my friends have got phones; they're always ringing each other.'

'That's just one extra bill to pay,' Father said.

'Come to think of it,' Mother said, 'we do need a phone, especially in an emergency.'

'I'll think about it,' Father said.

'Can I have a walkie-talkie please, Father?' Joshua said. 'All my friends have got walkie-talkies.'

'Can I have my ears pierced, please, Daddy?' Ruth asked. 'All my friends have got pierced ears and gold sleepers.'

Father handed Mother a brown envelope. 'I can't understand you children: the time you spend gallivanting around with friends, you could be reading your books, gaining knowledge. The more you read, the more you learn.'

'Oh, Father,' Ruth said. 'What's the good of reading a whole heap of books when I'm going to work in a bank?'

'Work in a bank!' Father repeated. 'Don't be

139

silly, child. You need a profession: lawyer, doctor, dentist . . .'

'Oh, Jasper,' Mother said. 'Stop foaming at the mouth.'

'Kiff, kiff, kiff,' Ruth giggled.

'You children take this thing for a joke,' Father said. 'Education is the only way you're going to climb the ladder.'

Mother interrupted, saying, 'Forget about climbing ladders, Jasper. We've got a letter here about climbing mountains. A skiing trip to Austria next Easter.'

Father said, 'That school is trying to bleed us dry.'

'You chose that school because you wanted me to mix with the right sort and get a good education, Father,' I said.

'I'm sorry, Hope,' Mother said. 'We can't afford it. One outing is enough. I've got to buy you new clothes for this party, and you'll have to take a card and a present, too.'

Father sighed. 'You children think money grows on trees.'

'Exactly!' Mother exclaimed.

Father smiled. 'Next Easter, eh?'

'What are you thinking, Jasper?' Mother asked.

'Well, it's not every day you get a chance to go skiing. I wouldn't mind going myself; sport of the élite,' Father said.

'Oh, it's not fair.' Ruth looked up. 'Hope's going skiing. Only last week Father said he couldn't afford to send Joshua and me on a day trip to Boulogne with our school.'

140

'It's not fair.' Joshua joined in.

'Not another word, miss lady, maasa man,' Father said. 'I haven't made a decision as yet.'

'That reminds me, Hope,' Mother said. 'I want you to help me defrost the fridge. There's so much ice in the frozen food compartment you need skis to get around.'

'Kiff, kiff, kiff . . .' Ruth and Joshua laughed.

As I sat polishing my silver spoon with care, my mind reeled back into the past: I watched Cousin Archie unearthing his treasures. I wondered why he and Aunt Jemima had singled me out, given me all those gifts? I kept them in my grip, treasured them. I was a lucky girl; not many children could say their palms had been crossed with a real silver spoon. I was proud of my treasures and I vowed to repay Cousin Archie and Aunt Jemima. I would get a good education and write about those old people one day.

I stared at my silver, bringing my mind back to the present: the gleam bounced off the cut-glass vase on the coffee table, throwing off rainbows. I thought of Sister Mary-Ann; my luck changed the moment she put her hand on my shoulder. I thought of Austria, skiing down the mountain side; I thought of Venetia's party, too. I was about to make new friends; hopefully we would all be going to Austria skiing next year. I was looking forward to the autumn term. I polished my silver with an urgency, stared at the cut-glass vase, the twinkling rainbows. I made a wish, but kept it to myself. Then I thought, I must start reading *Heidi* straight away.

13

Birds in the Wilderness

Dear Grandma,

Greetings to you and Grandpa. I must tell you something, Grandma: my visitor came, and it shamed me in front of the whole school. I had to walk across the dinner hall with the evidence on the back of my summer dress. But I feel fine now. There's a very nice nun called Sister Philippa. She explained to us, during one of her lessons, where babies come from. I've also got a little booklet that Sister Brigid, the school nurse, loaned me. It tells you all about 'periods' (the visitor). Sister Brigid gave me a letter to give Mother. I didn't wait for Mother to read it. I said, 'My period came today, Mother. Sister Philippa explained the facts of life to us, so there's no need to worry. But can I have some money to buy pads and an air letter, please? I want to write to Grandma.'

Mother said, 'My goodness, it seems like yesterday I left my little girl in Kingston. Now you've come of age. There's no need for you to buy any pads. I've been expecting this. There's a packet of Dr White's in your grip. I found the soiled panties in there, too, among your silver and a wad of notepaper with scribbles all over it; some nonsense about childhood.' I was embarrassed. I hung my head in shame.

Another piece of news, Grandma. There are two girls in my class who I really admire: Venetia and Amy. They befriended me the day my visitor shamed me. It was Venetia's birthday yesterday. She invited me to her birthday party. I made other friends, too. There's a Japanese girl in my class called Yoko. Once she saw her friends, Antonia and Jane, talking to me, she joined in, telling me to carry an extra pad in my satchel. It seems when you have a visitor there are lots of things you shouldn't do; everyone was advising me not to wash my hair, not to bath and not to go into the sea, for sharks love the smell of blood. They'll eat you. Anyway, we had lots of fun, playing party games.

Grandma, there's a wonderful nun at school called Sister Mary-Ann. She rushes around like a carefree goat-kid. She's going to be my form teacher next term, for Sister Julie has got sugar. (They call it diabetes over here.) She is retiring, and Sister Mary-Ann, who teaches English, Typing and Office Practice, will be taking her place. Sister Mary-Ann and Sister Agnes are organising a trip to Austria. Can you imagine a mountain top covered with snow, Grandma? Well, Austria is a cold mountainous country where it snows a lot. Father has promised to let me go. Venetia and Amy have been skiing before. We're all going to ski down the mountain side. I'm so excited, I can't wait for next Easter.

Grandma, I'm glad you liked the poem I sent you. I've written another one. Mother thinks it's nonsense. She went through my personal

belongings, saw it in my grip. I'll recite it for you;
just imagine you can hear my voice:

Childhood is full of expectations;
It is a time when we feel secure.
Often we enjoy visitations
And occasionally we feel insecure.

Childhood is full of occasions;
Everyone seems so sincere
And with all the invitations
How can we ever discover who's insincere.

Childhood is full of directions;
Everyone wants to impress.
Sometimes we offer explanations
But rarely do we ever confess.

Sister Mary-Ann says in the autumn term she's
going to organise a school magazine. We'll all be
encouraged to write articles, short stories and
poetry for the magazine. Sister Mary-Ann says the
writing has to be first class, so I'm working on my
grammar and punctuation. I'm going to submit the
two poems I've sent you. Do you think they're
good enough?
Anyway, nothing more to say, Grandma. I close
with love until I hear from you. Write soon.

Your same,
Hope.

August blazed into our lives, minus the cool breeze
we took for granted at home. Butterflies settled on
the parched grass in our garden, flapped their

wings; they never got up again. Insects carried them off. Ants went round and round the garden, gone mad under the heat of the sun. My cho-cho vine refused to crawl any further up the trunk of the barren apple tree; the leaves lay limply. Father uprooted it; said it wasn't being productive. I chewed my anger in silence.

It was late Friday evening. The family gathered round the television watching a Western, *Stagecoach*.

'What a day I've had.' Father fidgeted on the sofa. 'I almost threw in the rag. The boss asked me to move a mountain of files from the finance office into the basement, said he was happy for me to change into an overall because the files were covered with dust: my white shirt and tie were filthy after I'd finished taking the files down, pushing trolley after trolley load into the basement. I was so annoyed.'

'Guess what!' Mother said. 'Half of the girls are going on maternity leave and they're not coming back, including the supervisor. I've been offered the post of deputy supervisor.'

'Congratulations!' Father said. 'Every day carry bucket to the well, one day the bucket bottom must fall out.'

'The teacup in my case,' Mother said. 'I'm boiling up like a copper kettle. Some of the girls objected to my promotion and the supervisor said, "Girls, Beatrice has only been given this post because she's the eldest in the office: age before beauty . . ." Can you believe it?'

'Nothing surprises me nowadays, Bea,' Father

said. 'This calls for a celebration. I'll round up the boys.'

'I've still got a bottle of white rum in the cupboard,' Mother said. 'We'll toast the future.'

'So let it be written, so let it be done,' Father said.

The house next door, on our left, stood empty for the first few months of our arrival in London. But after Easter it was sold to a black couple with two children. The previous occupier was a couple who were sitting-tenants. When the wife died, the husband went into an old folks' home. The landlord had put the house up for sale. Father took a dislike to our new neighbours straight away: the head of the house wore a London Transport uniform and his wife wore a nurse's uniform. Their two daughters were installed in one of the local comprehensives.

Father met Mr Walker in the corner shop buying the *Sun* newspaper. Father read the *Daily Mail*, said you could tell a person by his reading matter: the Walkers were not in his league, quashies.

The summer holidays wore on. I watched enviously as the girls next door, Vivette and Yvette, played on the pavement or sat on the window-sill outside their house gossiping with friends. The girls had only been in the area two minutes, it seemed, yet they'd made lots of friends; at least half a dozen black girls called on them. When they were not racing each other down the street like unbridled horses, shouting, they showed off their dancing skills on the pavement. Father said the Walkers' girls had 'no home training'. We were not allowed to play with them.

Mother fared no better than Ruth and me. The lady of the house next door, Mrs Walker, was called Dorcas. She called Mother at the fence, said her husband, Lester, and some friends were throwing a pardner, they threw five pounds a week; each week one person drew seventy-five pounds a hand. That was how they saved the deposit to buy their house. Would Mother and Father care to join in? Mother said she'd ask Father. But no amount of pleading would change Father's mind. He preferred to put his money in the bank.

Mr Walker had all his friends round to play dominoes. Father was invited, he declined; said he didn't play dominoes. It was the first time our father had openly told a white lie. The Walkers got the message, said 'good morning', 'good evening', never mentioned dominoes and pardners again.

It was mid August. Father's friends came to celebrate Mother's promotion. They couldn't make it when Father had invited them. This was to be a belated celebration. Everyone settled in the sitting-room, complaining about the heat.

'I fancy a game of dominoes,' the travel agent said. 'Get your set out, Jasper.'

'I'll pass on that one,' Father said. 'My neighbour, London Transport, the one I told you about, invited me to play dominoes with him and his friends. What a laugh! The man's not in my league. He even invited Bea and me to join a pardner. They should put their money in the bank; if you don't have collateral in the bank you can't get a loan when you need it.'

The actor said, 'Very few banks are willing to lend black people money, Jasper. I don't blame them; you can't get a dime to borrow from the bank manager without collateral . . .'

The subject got round to the lack of relatives in this country; they were scattered all over the place. Some of them weren't ambitious enough; you couldn't mix with them.

That explained why Robin and his parents, Uncle Herman and Aunt Ione, hadn't been to see us. Father didn't want them around. They were British Rail and factory material.

'When is Robin coming to see us?' Ruth asked. 'We haven't seen him for years. I'm longing to see him.'

'How about a game of cards?' the boys said.

'When I was growing up.' Father shuffled the cards. 'I didn't mix with Herman. He wasn't in my class, had no head for books. He worked on Uncle Ely's farm when he left school. Then he got his ticket to England. He and his friends came to better themselves. I came because it was the trend . . .'

'Don't fib, Jasper. We came for the same reason as the others,' Mother said. 'All this nonsense about riff-raff.'

'You don't hold your head high enough, Bea,' Father said. 'You're too eager to embrace the world and its cousins!'

'God, you're unsociable, Jasper,' Mother snapped.

'Boys, black women have all the luck in this

country, unlike us,' Father said. 'We could work from now till Thy kingdom come and still we wouldn't get promotion.' He raised his glass: 'Congratulations, Bea, you're the breadwinner now.'

'You're impossible, Jasper,' Mother said. 'I'm going to see Dorcas.' She took Naomi and was about to walk out.

'You're not taking my child over there!' Father reared like an unbridled horse. 'You can go if you like, but I will not have Naomi mixing with quashies!' He wrestled with Mother.

'Calm down, Jasper.' The singer, who wore a beige bush jacket, held Father, reigned him in. 'No fisticuffs; not in front of the children. Shame on you, man.'

'Let me go, man.' Father blew hot. 'Let me go . . .'

'I won't be bullied by you, Jasper! I'm not a child. I'm going to see Bunty.' Mother walked out, taking a wailing Naomi with her, not giving us a second glance.

'Boys, you're lucky,' Father said, 'free, single and disengaged. You can come and go as you please. Lord, I hate this life. Why, if I were in Jamaica I'd be living like a lord now.' He caught our frowning faces. 'Right, off to your rooms. The boys and I want to talk in private.'

We sensed the thin elastic, our family, stretching to breaking point. Father voiced his regrets about coming to England. His voice travelled to the top of the stairs; we sat listening, heard things we shouldn't have heard.

'Can I sleep in your room, girls?' Joshua sat on

the bed. 'Like I used to do back home when I got scared.'

To tell the truth none of us could sleep: the quarrel had unsettled us and Father was downstairs spilling his heart.

Ruth got out of bed, stood by the window, staring at the night sky. She said, 'Remember how we used to count the stars in vain and watch the man in the moon?'

'Yes.' I felt so naïve. Only three weeks ago we'd watched Neil Armstrong's first step from Apollo 11 onto the moon. We thought heaven was on the moon. We'd expected to see the astronauts gathering round the throne of God, being greeted by the angels. We came down to earth when Neil Armstrong, the pilot, said, 'This is tranquility base. The eagle has landed.' When the hatch opened Armstrong began his descent. His feet touched the Moon-dust. 'That's one small step for man, one giant leap for mankind.'

Joshua and I joined Ruth, studying the heavens. We sang 'Here we sit like birds in the wilderness . . .'

Father's friends went home. He came up the stairs, snapping. 'Can't a man's ears eat grass in his own home! Hush up and go to sleep. Good night!'

'Good night, Father.'

Monday morning came, and Mother seemed to have forgotten the rotten weekend. She said, 'Aren't you going to work, Jasper? I hope you're not planning on taking refuge in that bed indefinitely?'

We children stood at the top of the stairs listening.

'Could be. I want a better life, Beatrice.'

'Suit yourself.' Mother went out.

'Hope, bring me a cup of black coffee!' Father commanded.

Little did we know that that afternoon was to be a turning point in our lives. There came a knock at the door.

'Send those children away from my door, Joshua!' Father shouted. 'Send them away, do you hear me?'

'Telegram for Mr Byfield,' the postman said.

'Send those children away . . .' Father repeated.

We children examined the telegram, hearts racing.

'Father, Father; telegram for you!'

Father came down in striped pyjamas, frowning. He took the flimsy paper, knitted his brow, tore it open. His Adam's apple moved. 'Lord, just when you ask for peace and safety, sudden destruction strikes: Herman is dead! What a trial. Ione wants me to call her straight away.'

'Cousin Herman is dead and we never got a chance to know him,' Ruth and Joshua said. 'Oh, Father.'

'Poor Robin,' I said. 'What will become of him now?'

'What's going on?' Mother walked through an open front door. (We'd forgotten to close it.) She held Naomi on her hip. 'I come home to find my baby crawling out the front door. What's going on? What have you children done now?'

Father handed Mother the telegram. 'Herman is dead, Bea.'

'Dear Lord!' Mother took the telegram, read it. 'Quick, Jasper! Go next door and ask Lester if you can use the telephone. He's just arrived home from work. He's on the early shift this week.' She readjusted sixteen-month-old Naomi's position, and hugged her to her bosom. 'Go on, Jasper.'

We children stared at Father's pained expression. He'd never had a civil conversation with our neighbours.

'What are you waiting for, Jasper?' Mother asked. 'Herman was your cousin; it's your responsibility.'

'I'm not dressed, Beatrice,' Father snapped. 'I will not have my neighbour seeing me in my pyjamas.'

'For heaven's sake, Jasper! This is an emergency. Who cares what you look like? Here, take Naomi.'

'Take Naomi, Hope,' Father said. 'I'm going to have a bath. Trust Herman to get himself killed: irresponsible.'

We children were scandalized by Father's lack of respect for the dead. And if we had held childhood memories of him, he fell off the pedestal for good.

By nightfall Father's friends gathered in the sitting-room where Uncle Herman's wanderings became public knowledge. It seemed he hadn't put aside a cent for the future, though he'd made it clear time and time again that he didn't want to be buried on foreign soil. Father being the nearest kin, Aunt Ione summoned him.

The story of Uncle Herman's life was told to Mother over the telephone. He had left Aunt Ione for a lady friend whom he met at work. They lived in a flat with their twin boys whom Uncle Herman was said to dote on. Aunt Ione worked round the clock, sewing dresses in a factory, to make ends meet. Robin was often left to mind his little brother Joel. The last time Aunt Ione and the children saw Uncle Herman, he'd asked for a divorce. On the way home he was involved in a head-on collision. Mother said Aunt Ione was really angry. She'd said, 'Vengeance is mine saith the Lord. Retribution! No way am I starving my children by spending our last farthing to send the carcass home. Let his new family foot the bill.'

Of course, Uncle Herman's common-law wife couldn't offer financial help. She lived in rented accommodation, had twin boys to take care of. Father said blood was thicker than water. We noticed how he shouldered his responsibility with enthusiasm as he discussed the problem of sending the body home with his friends. And someone had to accompany the body, too. The travel agent said he'd arrange the flight: Father and the coffin would leave from Manchester Airport in two days' time. The boys had a whip round. Father dipped into the emergency kitty. There was no money left.

Our neighbours, the Walkers, came over. They put Father to shame with their generosity.

'If dere's anything me can do, money-wise, Mr Byfield,' Mr Walker said, 'jus' say de wo'd. Me jus' get me 'and o' pardner. If you need any money, dohn 'esitate to ask.'

'Call me Jasper,' Father said. 'I'm all right, thanks.'

'If we need any extra,' Mother said hastily, 'we'll

call on you, Lester. Thanks very much.' The women left the room.

'Now! How about a game o' dominoes?' Mr Walker said.

All the men were happy to play. Mrs Walker prepared sandwiches in the kitchen. Her girls had gone to stay with relatives in Brixton. Mother was upstairs, putting Naomi to bed.

Father slammed a domino down on the table, humming: 'I'm coming home, I've done my time . . .'

The actor matched dominoes. 'I've applied for a job at JBC. With my background it's as good as mine. I'll be packing my bags very soon. Look me up anytime you're in JA, boys.'

The singer said, 'I'm thinking of going to America. I'm not staying in this God-forsaken place any longer. No way am I going home in a wooden box. No sir.'

'I'll be here till my pension comes up,' the dentist said.

'My business is just getting off the ground,' the travel agent said. 'I've met a nice secretary; time I settled down.'

Mother came down the stairs, opened the front door to Mrs Parsons, who'd been to Hampton Court on a day trip. They joined Mrs Walker in the kitchen. We children huddled together on the sofa, watching the domino players. I thought of Robin, that day long ago when we sat on the grass in the schoolyard. He'd been playing cricket and fretted about whether he'd make new friends in England. I wondered how things had turned out for him at school. I hoped it was better than his home life.

'Key domino,' Mr Walker shouted. 'Key domino!'

The singer and the actor stood round the domino table, waiting their turn. They hummed 'Island in the Sun'.

'Bwoy, Harry Belafonte can sing, sah,' Mr Walker said. 'Me raise me glass to 'im, man.'

'Good to see one of our people making the grade,' Father said. 'A successful black man. It gives you hope . . .'

I saw our island: the sun, the forests, the river and the funeral, too. There'd be weeping and wailing, and the gnashing of teeth, and clicking of tongues. The young men would shake their heads in anger. Uncle Herman had thrown away the opportunity they craved. I thought of Mr Trelawny, how he'd cautioned the children who were going abroad, told them to 'seize opportunity by the hand'. I knew I had to grasp education by the hand if I intended to be a writer, fulfil the promise I'd made to the old people at home. I thought of Sister Mary-Ann, my new form-teacher and remembered Grandma saying: 'Encouragement sweeten labour'. Sister Mary-Ann was the tonic I needed. My school life looked bright, but my home life was in jeopardy, and all I could do was watch and wait.

'New game,' Mr Walker said. 'Double six pose.'

'My card,' Father said. 'I've got a winning hand, boys. I'm not sitting this game out.'

'Cho, man,' the singer said. 'You always call the shots.'

155

'Some people are born to be losers and some are born to be winners,' Father joked. 'I'm a winner, boys.'

'Speaking of losers.' Mother entered the room, placing a tray on the coffee-table. 'I hope the house in Kingston hasn't devalued. Put it on the market when you go home, Jasper.'

'We're not selling it.' Father stared at the dominoes.

'What?' Mother demanded. 'But we need the money.'

'We'll discuss it later.' Father could have been addressing a child. 'Now is not the time, Beatrice.'

'Very well.' Mother's nostrils flared. 'So be it.'

The boys kept their eyes on the dominoes.

'What about my trip to Austria?' I asked.

'Look here, Hope,' Mother snapped: 'we're in the middle of a crisis and all you can think of is spreeing.'

'That's not fair,' I cried. 'Father, you promised!'

'Hold your tongue, Hope,' Father said. 'There's no money in the kitty. Anyway, there's more to life than skiing.'

The travel agent said, 'I've always fancied skiing in Switzerland. How much is the fare?'

'Yes,' the dentist and the singer said. 'How much . . .'

A frown clouded Father's face. 'Whoa, boys. You've done enough already. I don't know when I'll be able to repay you.'

'Oh, well, if you change your mind . . .' the actor said.

Mr Walker studied his dominoes, looked into Father's eyes. 'If its a question of money, Jasper.'

Father was poker-faced. 'Thanks, Lester, but I can't accept your offer. I don't want to accumulate any more debts.'

'Mother!' I cried. 'Father promised.'

'I can't discuss it now, Hope. I've got more important things on my mind.' She added, 'Go and pack your grips, children. We're going up to Manchester . . .'

'Do we have to?' Joshua tatted. 'I hate travelling.'

'So do I,' Ruth said. 'I never want to see those grips again. They remind me too much of the day Grandma received that air mail letter. Grandpa's legs gave way and he couldn't jig for us. Grandma kept packing and unpacking our grips for days, crying and humming. Now Ruth imitated Grandma's voice:

Take a grip, my brother,
Take a grip, another grip.
Hold fast and never look back.
No matter what the people of the world may
say:
Hold fast, my brother, hold fast . . .

'A born singer,' the musician said. 'You should let her audition for "Opportunity Knocks", Jasper.'

'A proper little actress, too,' the actor said. 'Send her to stage school, man.'

'There's no money in acting or singing, not for our people; she'll be sucking salt all her life,' Father said.

'There's hope for the younger generation, man.'

'Please, Father,' Ruth said. 'Please let me go to stage school. I don't want to work in a bank anymore. I want to be an actress or a singer.'

'Hold your tongue, miss lady,' Father snapped. 'I'll decide where your future lies . . .'

Once again the future seemed uncertain, for the packing of grips meant a new direction. Father slammed a domino down on the coffee table; the legs shook as the domino split asunder.

Mr Walker said seriously: 'What yuh tryin' to do, man; 'mash up de house?'

'So let it be written, so let it be done.' Father said in a commanding tone. Mother kissed her teeth. He gave her a great wink, but I couldn't help noticing there was a far-away look in his eyes: images of Father chopping down my cho-cho vine and smashing Ruth's doll's house crowded my vision. A feeling of uneasiness washed over me and I said to myself, 'Will we still be together this time next year?'

A Selected List of Fiction from Mammoth

While every effort is made to keep prices low, it is sometimes necessary to increase prices at short notice. Mandarin Paperbacks reserves the right to show new retail prices on covers which may differ from those previously advertised in the text or elsewhere.

The prices shown below were correct at the time of going to press.

☐	7497 2646 6	**The Face at the Window**	Vivien Alcock	£3.99
☐	7497 2067 0	**The Parsley Parcel**	Elizabeth Arnold	£3.99
☐	7497 2388 2	**Whispers in the Graveyard**	Theresa Breslin	£3.99
☐	7497 1794 7	**Born of the Sun**	Gillian Cross	£3.99
☐	7497 1066 7	**The Animals of Farthing Wood**	Colin Dann	£3.99
☐	7497 1823 4	**White Peak Farm**	Berlie Doherty	£3.50
☐	7497 0184 6	**The Summer House Loon**	Anne Fine	£3.99
☐	7497 0962 6	**The Away Team**	Michael Hardcastle	£2.99
☐	7497 0136 6	**I Am David**	Anne Holm	£3.99
☐	7497 1664 9	**Hiding Out**	Elizabeth Laird	£4.50
☐	7497 0791 7	**The Ghost of Thomas Kempe**	Penelope Lively	£3.99
☐	7497 2644 X	**The Voices of Silence**	Bel Mooney	£3.99
☐	7497 1754 8	**The War of Jenkins' Ear**	Michael Morpurgo	£3.99
☐	7497 0831 X	**The Snow Spider**	Jenny Nimmo	£3.99
☐	7497 0656 2	**Journey of 1000 Miles**	Ian Strachan	£3.99
☐	7497 2734 9	**Panther in Argyll**	Lisa Tuttle	£3.99
☐	7497 0796 8	**Kingdom by the Sea**	Robert Westall	£3.99

All these books are available at your bookshop or newsagent, or can be ordered direct from the address below. Just tick the titles you want and fill in the form below.

Cash Sales Department, PO Box 5, Rushden, Northants NN10 6YX.
Fax: 01933 414047 : Phone: 01933 414000.

Please send cheque, payable to 'Reed Book Services Ltd.', or postal order for purchase price quoted and allow the following for postage and packing:

£1.00 for the first book, 50p for the second; **FREE POSTAGE AND PACKING FOR THREE BOOKS OR MORE PER ORDER.**

NAME (Block letters)..

ADDRESS..

....

☐ I enclose my remittance for ....

☐ I wish to pay by Access/Visa Card Number ☐☐☐☐☐☐☐☐☐☐☐☐☐☐☐☐

Expiry Date ☐☐☐☐

Signature ....

Please quote our reference: MAND